"I'll hold

Travis transferred the baby into Gwen's arms, and the little girl laid her head trustingly on her shoulder. Gwen's heart swelled with pleasure as she brushed a kiss against the baby's velvet cheek.

"Perfect," Travis murmured as he wrapped his arms around Gwen and Elizabeth, leading them into a slow, swaying dance.

It should have been harmless. But Gwen hadn't counted on having to look directly into Travis's eyes while they moved to the music. She didn't want him to know he was arousing her, but those eyes probably saw everything—her rapid breathing, her beating pulse, her flushed skin.

"Let me love you, Gwen," he whispered softly.

His mouth was beautiful, she thought. Every woman should have a chance to kiss a mouth like that once in her life. And if the rest of him lived up to the sensuous promise of his mouth...

She was putty in his hands, and she knew it. "I don't want to be another notch in your belt," she said in an effort to break the spell he was weaving over her.

Travis smiled, slow and sexy, his eyes alight with banked passion. "Then let me be a notch in yours...."

Dear Reader,

Cowboys have a reputation for being fearless. Ride a big, bad bronc—no problem. Turn back a thundering herd—piece of cake. But make a cowboy responsible for one tiny baby girl and he trembles in his boots. It's positively adorable.

Last month, in *The Colorado Kid*, I subjected rancher Sebastian Daniels to that fate. This month, lady-killer Travis Evans gets his turn with baby Elizabeth, who may or may not be his child. Travis decides she is and stakes his claim by naming her Lizzie.

That makes two cowboys so far who each think they're the baby's father. A third prospective daddy shows up in Book 3 of the miniseries, *Boone's Bounty*, available next month. And in September, a Single Title brings the series to a rousing finish as Nat Grady arrives in town proclaiming *That's My Baby!* Nat turns the baby battle into quite a rodeo. Come watch!

Warmly,

Vicki Lewis Thompson

Vicki Lewis Thompson
TWO IN THE SADDLE

HARLEQUIN®

TORONTO • NEW YORK • LONDON
AMSTERDAM • PARIS • SYDNEY • HAMBURG
STOCKHOLM • ATHENS • TOKYO • MILAN • MADRID
PRAGUE • WARSAW • BUDAPEST • AUCKLAND

To Julie Kistler,
for generously sharing her invisible,
chanting gnomes when I needed a creative boost.

ISBN 0-373-25884-4

TWO IN THE SADDLE

Copyright © 2000 by Vicki Lewis Thompson.

WEDDINGS MADE Travis Evans nervous.

Standing at the altar of the Huerfano Community Church with his good buddy Sebastian Daniels was like hanging out with a guy who had chicken pox. One wrong move on Travis's part and bam! He'd catch the marriage bug. And that would mean the end of life as he knew it.

But somebody had to be there for Sebastian. By rights Sebastian should have had four guys lined up to give him moral support, but he and Matty hadn't been willing to wait for folks to rearrange their schedules.

Sebastian's brother Ed was stuck in Alaska, and as for the three cowboys who made up Sebastian's inner circle, only Travis was available. Nat Grady was overseas working in a small, war-torn country with a name Travis had trouble pronouncing. Boone Conner was on the road in New Mexico with his mobile horseshoeing business and tracking him down had been impossible.

So Travis was Sebastian's best man, which was just as well, Travis thought, because that balanced out the wedding party. Matty's family hadn't been able to make it on such short notice, either, so her only attendant was Gwen Hawthorne, maid of honor. Or matron. Travis wasn't sure which it was when a woman was divorced. Divorced and marriage-shy. It was a hell of a promising combination, in Travis's opinion. Too bad Gwen hated his guts.

Even though Sebastian and Matty were light in the wedding-party department, they weren't short of wedding guests. The tiny clapboard church was packed. The men had dusted off their best Western-cut suits, and the women.... Travis sighed with longing. The women looked like a bouquet of Colorado wildflowers in their pastel-colored outfits. The air was still cool on this May afternoon, but the women of Huerfano had dressed for spring.

Travis loved how warmer weather invited the ladies to bare a little more of their delectable skin, and ordinarily he would have taken delight in the number of eligible females within range of his smile. But weddings were a dangerous time to flirt. Weddings gave single women *ideas*.

The minister, Pete McDowell, had been a hell-raiser in his youth according to what Travis had heard, but he'd entered the ministry and reformed. With his neatly trimmed gray beard and long robe, he looked like the sort of person who could tie the knot good and tight.

Besides, everybody agreed Pete had been born with a voice that belonged either in the pulpit or on the radio. He turned now and nodded toward the church organist, Sarah Jane Ashfelder, who began to play.

Out of habit, Travis glanced over and winked at her. She blushed and bobbled a chord. Immediately he regretted the wink, partly because he'd flustered her and partly because everybody in the valley knew Sarah Jane was desperately seeking a husband. A wink from him while Sarah Jane was playing the organ at a wedding gave the wrong impression all the way around.

"Got the ring?" Sebastian whispered out of the corner of his mouth.

It was about the hundredth time Sebastian had asked since this morning, but Travis cut him some slack. A guy had a right to be wrecked on his wedding day. "Yeah, I've got it," he murmured. "How're you holding up?"

"Shaking like a newborn calf."

"This is a good move, Sebastian." Travis thoroughly believed that. Even though he wasn't interested in matrimony himself, it fit some guys like a glove. Sebastian was one of those guys. And Matty Lang was perfect for him.

"I know it's a good move," Sebastian said softly. "But I'm no good at public displays like this. This collar itches, and my coat's too tight across the shoulders. I—"

A baby's loud wail rose above the deep tones of the organ. The congregation turned toward the back of the church, their murmurs of curiosity getting louder as they strained to see where the noise was coming from.

"That would be Lizzie, kicking up a fuss in the vestibule," Travis said. "I knew it was a mistake, making her part of this shindig."

"It is *not* a mistake," Sebastian said in a low voice, although he could have spoken normally and not been heard above the bellowing organ, the screaming baby and the excited chatter of the guests. This baby had been the subject of much speculation, and folks were obviously dying to see her.

"She's not even four months old," Travis pointed out. "That's too little to be in a wedding."

"No, it's not. She's advanced for her age. Besides, Elizabeth brought Matty and me together. She belongs here. We forgot the pacifier, is all. I want my daughter to be part of this."

Travis felt like strangling Sebastian with his string tie. The guy wouldn't give up his wrongheaded insistence that he was Lizzie's father. "She's not your daughter. She's mine, as you damned well know." Travis was dead sure about it. The evidence was in the note he'd received three weeks ago in Utah, a note he'd now memorized.

> Dear Travis,
> I'm counting on you to be a godfather to my daughter Elizabeth until I can return for her. Your playful approach to life is just what she needs right now. I've left her with Sebastian at the Rocking D. Believe me, I wouldn't do this if I weren't in desperate circumstances.
>
>   In deepest gratitude,
>   Jessica

Lizzie was his, all right. Maybe he couldn't remember the specifics of that night when he, Sebastian, Boone and Jessica had celebrated the anniversary of their escape from an avalanche, but he was the likely candidate for fatherhood.

He recalled that all the guys had been drunk, drunk enough to make passes at Jessica, even though she was only a friend. And like a good friend, she'd driven them back to their cabin and tucked each of them in bed. He remembered her leaning over him, a smile on her face. He must have coaxed her in there with him, and that was when Lizzie had been conceived.

And yes, Sebastian had received a similar note asking him to be a godfather when Jessica left the baby on his doorstep. But Sebastian wasn't the type to get wasted and make love without protection. Travis hadn't ever done that before, either, but it wasn't out of the realm of possibility for him the way it was for Sebastian.

Nevertheless, Sebastian had taken credit for that baby and wouldn't give up. He was presently glaring at Travis, his jaw clenched. "She's my baby. She's got the Daniels nose."

"In your dreams. She looks exactly like a picture of my mother at that age."

Sarah Jane launched into the wedding march, pulling out all the stops to drown out the baby's cries.

"Oh, yeah?" Sebastian said. "Then I guess I never showed you a picture of *my* mother at that age. She—"

"Gentlemen." Pete McDowell lifted his eyebrows in censure. "I don't think this is the time or the place to argue your paternity issues. The processional has begun."

Sebastian gulped and faced the back of the church.

Travis turned in that direction, too. Sure enough, here came Gwen pushing the antique baby buggy she'd unearthed from the attic of her Victorian house. People on both sides of the aisle craned their necks hoping for a glimpse of the mystery baby that two men claimed to have fathered.

Gwen had pushed Lizzie down the aisle in the buggy during the rehearsal, and the little girl had seemed to love it. But today was a different story, apparently. Today Lizzie was having nothing to do with that buggy.

Gwen had decorated it with flowers and ribbons so it looked real pretty, and she'd found a way to hook her bridal bouquet onto the buggy handle. Lizzie didn't seem to appreciate any of Gwen's efforts. But it wasn't the buggy decorations that held Travis's gaze. One glimpse of Gwen and his hormones snapped to attention.

She wore a dress the same color as new aspen leaves, and the pale green looked amazing against her golden skin. He vaguely remembered hearing that she had Cheyenne ancestors somewhere in her family tree. That also explained her jet-black hair, worn up today in some elaborate arrangement that mystified and tantalized him. She'd woven green ribbons and flowers through her shiny curls, making her look like a Native American princess—a modern princess who knew her way around a curling iron.

Travis licked his lips. He was of the firm belief that women spent all that time putting their hair up hoping that some man would itch to take it down. And he did.

The sleeves of her dress were long, with little conservative buttons at the wrists, but the neckline wasn't even remotely conservative. Travis stared at the most spectacular cleavage he'd seen in a coon's age. He sighed as he calculated the odds of ever enjoying that bounty. She was the only single woman in the valley he hadn't been able to charm.

And that frustrated him, especially at this moment when Gwen was walking toward him displaying her wares so effectively. Travis was relatively unacquainted with frustration, considering that women seemed to enjoy giving him what he wanted when he wanted it.

Because he was used to having his needs satisfied in short order, he'd never realized that rejection could be a more powerful aphrodisiac than acceptance. Good thing these fancy pants Sebastian had rented for him had pleats.

Gwen held her head high and smiled as she pushed the buggy containing the screaming baby, but Travis noticed the tension around her eyes. And then, for one electric moment, her dark gaze met his. Her silent plea for help might have been unconscious, but it was unmistakable.

Without thinking, Travis reacted. He crossed in front of Sebastian and the minister and met Gwen as she reached the altar.

She paused, and her eyes widened as he lifted a squalling Lizzie out of the buggy and cradled her against the shoulder of his tux.

They'd decked the baby out in a white eyelet dress and white booties, which was reasonable, but some idiot had decided to torment her by putting a bow on an elastic band around her head. No wonder she was upset. Travis took the bow off and kissed the little girl's damp cheek.

Gwen cleared her throat. "Travis—"

"Go on over to your spot," Travis murmured, tucking the bow gizmo in his pocket. "I'll handle her."

"But—"

"Go on. I'll get her to stop." And in fact he already had. Lizzie snuffled against his shoulder and grabbed on to his lapel as if she didn't plan to let go. He smiled at Gwen. "See?"

Gwen shook her head. "Unreal," she muttered.

He shrugged. "Most girls like me." With a wink at Gwen he returned to his place holding Lizzie.

Gwen didn't want to be touched by the picture of Travis standing at the altar letting a baby slobber on his tux. On her way to the front of the church, in addition to worrying about Elizabeth's crying, she'd noticed that Travis looked like a god up there. She'd known he was mouth-watering in jeans, but she hadn't been prepared for the sight of him in a tux.

Because she loved everything Victorian, she had a weakness for a man in a tuxedo, a man who looked as if he'd stepped out of another era. Dressing Travis in a tie and tails and setting him smack-dab in front of her should be against the law.

She'd nearly forgotten Elizabeth's wailing as she took in the allure of the high, white collar emphasizing his strong neck, the black coat stretched tight across his broad shoulders, and the snug fit of his dove-gray vest. Vests were made for men built like Travis. The delicate pink rosebud in his lapel only emphasized his virility.

In order to get her hormones under control, she'd convinced herself that Travis was vain as a peacock. She visualized him preening in front of the mirror, combing his rich brown hair, gazing into the tawny depths of those bedroom eyes of his and winking at his reflection before he walked out to face his admirers. But a peacock wouldn't let a baby suck on the shoulder of his coat. A peacock wouldn't let that same baby pull on his string tie until it came undone. A peacock wouldn't have come to Gwen and Elizabeth's rescue in the first place.

The organ music swelled, and with some effort Gwen turned her gaze away from Travis and Elizabeth in order to give Matty the respect and attention she deserved.

Matty came down the aisle, regal in the simple white gown Gwen had insisted she wear, despite this being a second marriage. Gwen had advised her on the flowers, too, and the old-fashioned bouquet of rosebuds, lavender and ivy was exactly right for Matty. Watching her, Gwen felt her throat tighten with happiness, pride, and a trace of longing.

Her friend had never looked more radiant. The expression of pure love on Matty's face made Gwen yearn for something she hadn't wished for in a very long time—a love of her own. Both she and Matty had hooked up with scoundrels the first time around, but Matty hadn't let that stop her from dreaming. Now she had a man who would lay down his life for her.

Gwen swallowed the lump in her throat. Men like Sebastian Daniels were rare, and she knew it. The rancher's good looks could have served him well as a lady-killer, but instead he was humble, sweet, and adorably dense about the effect he had on women. He was the exact opposite of Travis, who was all too aware that women swooned when he walked by.

But Gwen would not swoon. By God, she would not swoon.

As Matty joined Sebastian at the altar, Gwen sneaked a peek at Travis to see how he was getting along with Elizabeth. He was rumpled and damned sexy-looking from dealing with the baby. He'd removed his boutonniere, probably so Elizabeth wouldn't stick herself on the pin or try to eat the rosebud. Gwen was impressed with his caution.

Continuing to keep the baby entertained, he played nosey-nosey with her, and she chuckled, a low sound of feminine delight. No doubt about it, Travis had a way with the fairer sex, regardless of age.

On a hunch, Gwen glanced around the small church. The men were watching the ceremony. But as she'd expected, the women, ranging from eight to eighty, were watching Travis. From their expressions of open adoration, Gwen figured Travis would be booked up for the rest of the summer on the basis of this one little scene.

Well, good. The busier he was, the less chance she'd have of running into him. And she wanted to steer clear of Travis Evans. She certainly did. Definitely. The sexual tingle she felt every time she looked at him would go away eventually, especially if she didn't have to look at him very often. This wedding would be the worst of it. After today, she'd have clear sailing.

But today was a challenge, because she caught herself constantly glancing over at Travis, right along with every other woman in the church. He was strong medicine, especially with that baby.

Maybe he realized the baby was a terrific prop. That thought gave her some comfort. If he was using the baby to get women's attention, then that made him...calculating. She had no use for a calculating man. Yes, he probably had ulterior motives for holding Elizabeth. What a grandstander, playing with that baby and making every woman in the place drool.

"Gwen," Matty whispered.

Gwen blinked.

"The ring," Matty said, her tone amused.

Hot embarrassment flooded through Gwen. She'd lost her place in the proceedings. "Coming right up," she murmured as she reached in the buggy, found the small box she'd put there and took out the ring. She'd planned to have it ready and waiting when the time came, but she'd become so absorbed with Travis, she'd blown her assignment. Damn that tuxedo-wearing, baby-holding cowboy, anyway.

With new determination she focused on Sebastian and Matty. From her position she could only see the back of Matty's head, golden curls covered in white tulle. But with her height advantage she could peer right over Matty and watch Sebastian's face.

And sure enough, he was giving his new bride *The Look*. Gwen couldn't define it exactly, but it was a potent combination of love, respect, devotion, lust, appreciation, and a few more emotions she hadn't identified yet. Sebastian's expression left no doubt in anyone's mind that Matty was his one and only.

The lump returned to Gwen's throat. If she were completely honest with herself, she'd have to say that no one, not even her ex, had ever given her *The Look*. She wondered if she'd go through life without ever experiencing such a moment.

Pull yourself together she lectured herself. *Count your blessings*. She lived in a gem of a Victorian house and had been lucky enough to keep it after the divorce by opening a bed and breakfast. It turned out she loved the business, although at times she wondered if caring for her guests only took the place of caring for the family she'd always wanted.

But the house gave her roots. The itinerant life of her archeologist parents wasn't for her, and she'd hated the constant moving as a child. She tallied each year spent in Huerfano with pride, and she was now up to seven, more years than she'd ever stayed in one place in her life.

Maybe running a B&B didn't stack up well against her parents' international reputation, or her brother's prestigious job running a museum in Boston. Maybe they sometimes reminded her that she was twenty-nine and hadn't done anything with her life. But she wasn't giving up her house, no matter what anybody said.

"You may kiss the bride," Pete McDowell said.

A collective sigh went up from the congregation as Sebastian lifted Matty's veil and cupped her face in his big rancher's hands.

The tender moment lasted long enough to bring a mist of tears to Gwen's eyes. Then Elizabeth began chortling and wiggling in Travis's arms.

Scene-stealer, Gwen thought, and she wasn't sure whether she meant Elizabeth or Travis. She wondered what would happen with that little baby. Her mother, Jessica Franklin, seemed to be on the run from something or someone and wanted her daughter out of danger. Jessica had been gone for six weeks, long enough for Matty and Sebastian to bond with Elizabeth.

Personally, Gwen figured Travis was the baby's father, not Sebastian. But in the event Jessica never returned, Sebastian and Matty would provide a better home for the little girl than a playboy like Travis. Even Travis agreed on that point. Still, he seemed quite possessive of the baby and argued every time Sebastian tried to claim paternity.

But neither of them would find out who was Elizabeth's father until Jessica chose to tell them. She'd called a few times to check on Elizabeth, but she'd never stayed on the line long enough to answer any questions.

Gwen had never encountered something this strange, but maybe Jessica knew what she was doing. Elizabeth was safe and surrounded by people who loved her, including Gwen, although she was trying not to get too attached.

She'd learned detachment during a childhood of constant moving, losing both friends and familiar surroundings. So she'd kept in mind that Jessica could appear at any time and take the baby away, although she might have a fight on her hands at this point. Even from Travis. And he was good with the baby, Gwen admitted grudgingly. Still, he couldn't be counted on. Not in the long run.

"I give you Mr. and Mrs. Sebastian Daniels," Pete McDowell said in his deep, booming voice.

The congregation broke into applause and Sarah Jane launched into the recessional.

Gwen blinked back tears as Matty and Sebastian walked back down the aisle, arm in arm. She was so happy for her friend. And maybe a little sorry for herself, but she'd get over it.

Then she looked across at Travis. With sentiment running high at this moment, she was in no shape to deal with him, but deal with him she must.

It wouldn't be for long. A walk down the aisle, a dance at the reception, and she'd be free of her obli-

gation to fraternize with him. And it would be good
riddance.

She pushed the buggy toward the center aisle. As
Travis met her there with Elizabeth, Gwen inclined
her head toward the buggy, indicating Travis could
put Elizabeth back inside.

"I don't want to risk it," he murmured.

"Suit yourself." Pushing the buggy required two
hands. During rehearsal they'd linked arms and each
put a hand on the wooden handle to push the buggy
back down the aisle.

But that wouldn't work now. Travis couldn't hold
the baby, link arms with Gwen, and lend a hand pushing the buggy, so Gwen decided they could forego
linking arms. Just as well.

She used both hands to push the buggy, expecting
Travis to simply fall in step beside her. Instead he
shifted Elizabeth to his outside arm and slipped his
free arm around Gwen's waist. Instantly her heart
started chugging like a freight train.

"That's not necessary," she said, a smile pasted on
her face for the benefit of the congregation. Looks of
envy came shooting at her from all sides.

"Yes, it is."

"No, it's not." She tried to ease away. She was entirely too close to him and his spicy aftershave, especially after she'd just witnessed the emotional joining
of her two best friends.

"Yes, it is." His grip tightened at her waist, sending
shock waves all through her body. "We're supposed
to look as if we're together."

"Casually together, not plastered together." Oh, but

his hand felt good right there. She registered the imprint of each of his fingers through the soft material of her dress.

"Take it easy, sweetheart."

"I am most definitely *not* your sweetheart." And if her nerves jumped at his words, that was only because nobody had spoken an endearment to her in a while.

"Too bad for both of us. Listen, I know you hate me and this is torture for you, but we're almost done."

Oh, it was torture, all right. Torture of the highest order. And how she wished that hate was the emotion she was feeling for this man.

2

TRAVIS HAD ACTED on impulse, tucking Gwen against him as they proceeded up the aisle. Pure devilment had made him do it, probably, knowing how much she loathed him. Funny, though, once they were hip to hip, he felt her tremble.

He recognized that tremble. Women tended to do that when he touched them, but he wouldn't have expected that reaction from Gwen, who'd let him know she wasn't even slightly interested.

So when she started squawking about his behavior he held her tighter, to test her reaction to increased contact. Sure enough, that quiver got worse, and her skin flushed pink.

He noticed the color in her cheeks, and because he was a healthy male animal, he also noticed the color spread to the swell of her breasts above the green material of her dress. The way he figured it, if a woman chose to wear a neckline like that, she could expect a man to look his fill. He indulged for as long as he dared, which was only a few seconds, considering he and Gwen were in a very public place.

When he forced himself to look away, he was trembling a bit himself. Fantasies of unzipping her dress and sampling those generous breasts swirled through his mind, affecting his breathing.

She wasn't breathing so easy herself, and her agitation stirred up the erotic, cinnamon-flavored perfume she wore, which excited him even more. By the time they reached the back of the church and moved through the doors into the vestibule where Matty and Sebastian stood waiting, Travis had decided it might be worth his time to cut through the barbed wire Gwen had strung around herself to keep him out.

So what if he wasn't husband material? He'd taught several women that good sex didn't have to lead to everlasting love. Mutual enjoyment was justification enough for climbing between the sheets, in his opinion. Gwen needed to expand her options, and he was the guy to help her. If Lizzie hadn't been twisting his ear during the entire walk down the aisle, it would have been an outstanding interlude.

If he'd had any doubt about Gwen's reaction to him, she erased it once they passed through the main chapel doors. She wrenched away from him as if she'd been cuddled up to a hot stove. An indifferent woman wouldn't have made such a big production out of escaping.

Avoiding his gaze, she abandoned the buggy and rushed over to hug Matty. "I'm so happy for you!" she said.

Travis knew Gwen's sentiments were sincere, but there was a quivery edge to her voice, as if she might not be in complete control of herself. That pleased him. After their walk down the aisle, he'd had to take a few deep breaths, himself. He caught Matty looking at him over Gwen's shoulder, and he shrugged.

Then he pried Lizzie's fingers from his ear before walking over and holding out his hand to Sebastian. "Well, it's too late to turn back now, buddy."

Sebastian was grinning all over as he clasped Travis's hand. "We really did it, didn't we?"

"I do believe you did. Congratulations. You roped yourself a keeper." He turned to Matty, who looked happier than he'd ever seen her. He'd been her head wrangler at the Leaning L through the bad years with Butch, and the lonely years after Butch crashed his plane into a mountain. Technically she was his boss, but he loved her like a sister, and he was pleased as punch that she and Sebastian had finally figured out they were meant to be more than good neighbors.

Continuing to balance Lizzie in one arm, he leaned down and gave Matty a kiss on the cheek. "I hope you know you've hitched up with the stubbornest cowpoke in the valley," he murmured. "If he gives you any problems, let me know and I'll kick his butt for you."

"I'll keep that in mind," Matty said, her blue eyes twinkling.

"Nice going, Travis." Sebastian clapped him on the back. "I had Matty convinced I was perfect, but you had to open your yap and ruin my image."

"My pleasure." Travis smiled, then winced as Lizzie crowed happily, grabbed his nose and pinched hard. "The kid's got the instincts of a steer wrestler," he said as he peeled her fingers away.

Matty laughed. "I've taught her all she knows. I'm hoping she'll have that nose thing perfected by the time she's eighteen."

Travis figured now wasn't the time to mention there was a chance Lizzie wouldn't grow up on the Rocking D. Matty was more attached to this baby than she knew. "She's got the nose thing perfected now," he said, grabbing Lizzie's hand before she could latch on again.

Matty held out her arms. "Let me hold her while we take care of this reception line business. You've been tortured enough."

"That's a matter of opinion," Gwen said.

Travis shot her a look. The old defiance was back in her dark eyes, but he wasn't intimidated by it anymore. Underneath all her bluster was a woman aching to be kissed, and kissed well. He wondered if he might find the opportunity to take care of that before the night was out.

"Lizzie's okay with me," Travis said. "She'll be fine, now that we got rid of that bow apparatus."

"I knew that bow was a bad idea," Matty said, glancing at her new husband, "but Sebastian insisted on making her look like a girl."

"I *liked* the bow," Sebastian said, a stubborn gleam in his eye.

"Well, she didn't," Matty said. "And I'm proud of her for sticking to her guns." She turned back to Travis. "Hand over that little dickens. I miss her already."

Travis eyed Matty's white dress. He had a rough idea what the dress cost, and he'd heard some talk about keeping it for the next generation of brides in the Daniels family. He didn't think Lizzie's baby drool would improve the dress any. "I'll hang on to her. That outfit of yours is a keepsake, and this tux is only rented. Might as well keep the mess concentrated in one spot."

Matty looked down at her dress. "You have a point. I'm not used to being dolled up like this, and I keep forgetting I have to be careful." She smiled at Travis. "Thank you for your sacrifice. You saved the day."

"Sacrifice?" Gwen said. "Ha. He eats this stuff with a spoon. He—"

"Maybe we'd better set up our reception line," Matty said quickly. "People are heading this way. Gwen, you'll be first, then Travis, then Sebastian, then—"

"*There's* that adorable baby!" shrieked Donna Rathbone, kindergarten teacher and one of Travis's former girlfriends.

Donna had called him her teacher's pet, he remembered. He had fond memories of hot summer nights about two years ago. Donna hurried through the double doors of the main chapel and headed straight for him, followed by half the congregation, all female, and all jabbering about the baby.

"Then again, maybe we should put Travis first in line," Matty said as the women enveloped him in a sea of pastels and perfume.

MATTY AND Sebastian had decided to hold the reception inside a large tent on the Rocking D, and from Gwen's vantage point at the head table, the whole town seemed to be packed inside the tent's white canvas walls. Tiny clear lights strung from the tent poles sparkled in celebration and centerpieces of spring flowers bloomed on each linen-covered table. The bar was open and the buffet table was crowded with food.

Sensual pleasures teased Gwen from all sides—succulent barbecued beef and rich red wine, the seductive beat of a country tune, the scent of juniper every time the breeze lifted a tent flap a few inches. And then there was Travis in his rumpled tux, an attraction more compelling than the bride and groom, apparently.

Women surrounded him constantly, whether he happened to be holding Elizabeth or not. He was a very busy man as he tended to his many admirers, and yet every few minutes he'd pause, find Gwen in the throng, and send her a smile or a wink.

She tried to be unaffected...and failed. It was heady stuff to be singled out by the man who was clearly adored by every woman in the room. But the dinner part of the reception had nearly ended, and soon the dancing would begin, which meant she'd be expected to dance with Travis. And no matter how seductive the atmosphere, no matter how appealing the man, she must not give in to his considerable charms.

She'd known Travis would be trouble the first day she'd laid eyes on him while paying a visit to Matty's ranch. About four years earlier, she and Matty had met over the yarn counter at Coogan's Department Store and discovered they both had a passion for weaving. Their friendship had blossomed.

Gwen had taken up the craft as a way to heal after her divorce from Derek. Eventually she discovered that Matty used her floor loom as therapy while she dealt with an unhappy marriage, which gave the two women even more in common.

They enjoyed each other's company tremendously, and the only fly in the ointment had been Gwen's occasional forced interaction with Matty's head wrangler. Travis reminded her way too much of Derek. He pushed all the same buttons Derek had, making her pulse race with a look, her breath catch with a devilish grin. But Gwen had no intention of losing her heart to another rascal too handsome for his own good.

Fortunately Travis spent winters at his place in Utah, which meant Gwen only had to deal with him during the summer. Because summer was high season at Hawthorne House, she was usually too busy to socialize much. She'd been so subtle about avoiding Travis that even Matty hadn't known of her vulnerability until recently...until Elizabeth had turned all their lives topsy-turvy.

The baby was presently sitting on Sebastian's lap while Matty played patty-cake with her. Gwen smiled at the picture they made. No doubt about it, Elizabeth had totally changed Matty and Sebastian's life, fortunately for the better. But Matty and Sebastian belonged together. Gwen and Travis did not, and she'd be wise to keep that firmly in mind.

Travis returned to his place at the head table just as the band finished a tune. He signaled to the band, picked up his wineglass and raised it. "Ladies and gentlemen, may I have your attention?"

That would be no problem for the ladies, Gwen thought. At the sound of Travis's rich baritone, they'd all turned toward him like daisies to sunlight.

"I'd like to propose a toast to the bride and groom." He grinned. "You know, this is gonna be like shooting fish in a barrel, Sebastian."

"Roast him, Travis!" called one of the ranchers from a table in the back of the room.

Gwen rolled her eyes. Travis would make a joke of this, the way he made a joke of everything.

"Well, you folks ain't heard nothin' until you've heard Sebastian Daniels croon *Ghost Riders in the Sky*," Travis said. "If I'd been writing your vows, buddy, I would've made Matty promise to love, cherish, and put up with a round of *Ghost Riders* every blessed morning in the shower. Oh, and I don't want to forget the yodeling. Did you tell her about that, yet?"

Gwen laughed along with everyone else, including Matty and Sebastian.

Travis cleared his throat and Gwen prepared herself for more jokes.

But Travis was no longer smiling, and his tone had changed. "Yodeling aside, I've known Sebastian Daniels for a lot of years, and he's one hell of a friend. If you're in trouble, this is the man to call. His heart's bigger than the whole Sangre de Cristo range."

Gwen stared at Travis. Just when she thought she knew what to expect from him, he did the exact opposite.

"Sebastian loves this land," Travis said. "Until recently, I didn't think he could love anything, or anyone, more than this paradise he calls the Rocking D. But I was wrong. His fondness for this ranch is a drop in the bucket compared to the way he feels about the woman sitting next to him."

Emotion clogged Gwen's throat. She could take anything from Travis except heartfelt sincerity.

"And he's found his soul mate in Matty," Travis continued. "Matty is true-blue, the straightest shooter I've ever known. If there is such a thing as a match made in heaven, you're looking at it. God bless, Matty and Sebastian. I'm proud to be here."

Gwen was destroyed. She clapped furiously and blinked back tears. Then she took a quick sip of wine to toast the newlyweds and grabbed a napkin to dab at her eyes.

The band started playing a waltz, and Sebastian handed Elizabeth to Travis. "Thanks," he said, his voice suspiciously hoarse. "That was...damned nice."

"Outstanding," Matty said, sniffing.

"I meant every word," Travis said. "Now go have that first dance, Mr. and Mrs. Daniels. You deserve it." He sat down next to Gwen and propped Elizabeth on his lap. "What'd you think?" He sounded as if he actually cared.

"Great." Gwen took another gulp of her wine and choked on it. She snatched up her napkin again and held it over her mouth while she coughed.

"Easy, now." With one arm wrapped around Elizabeth, he leaned over and patted Gwen on the back. "Didn't mean to make you nervous."

She glanced at him. The hell he didn't. At least she had an excuse for the tears in her eyes as she continued to cough and gasp for breath.

"And now let's have the best man and the maid of honor on the floor," announced the band leader.

Travis leaned closer. "Are you up to it?"

She coughed once more. "Sure," she said hoarsely. "But what about Elizabeth?"

"We'll take her along." He stood and pulled back Gwen's chair.

Stupid her, she was disappointed that they were taking Elizabeth. What a dope she was, feeling sorry because she wouldn't have Travis all to herself. She was twenty times safer if they danced with Elizabeth cradled between them, and safety was important. Self-preservation was imperative.

Unfortunately Travis's speech had derailed her protective instincts and stirred up needs she would do well to bury, especially when she was around this man.

Travis guided her with a hand at her elbow as they wound through the tables to the dance floor. Once again Gwen became aware of the envy coming at her in waves. She and Travis would dance this one, obligatory number. After that, he'd be mobbed and she wouldn't have to worry about protecting herself from his advances. She should be happy about that, not depressed.

"How about if you hold Lizzie?" Travis asked as they stepped onto the temporary dance floor that had been erected in one corner of the tent. "Then I can hold both of you." Without waiting for an answer, he transferred the baby neatly into Gwen's arms.

Elizabeth was growing limp and her eyes drooped with fatigue.

Gwen cradled the little girl in her arms, and with a yawn Elizabeth laid her head trustingly on Gwen's shoulder and closed her eyes. Gwen's heart swelled with pleasure as she turned her head and brushed a kiss against the baby's velvet cheek.

In the past few weeks, Gwen had tried to keep some distance from this cherub, but she was afraid that distance had just disappeared. She'd fallen in love with the baby like everyone else who came within Elizabeth's charmed circle. If Elizabeth ever left Huerfano, the town would be wall-to-wall with broken hearts.

"Perfect," Travis murmured, as he wrapped his arms around Gwen and Elizabeth and gently led them into a slow, swaying dance.

The baby sighed and gave in to sleep, relaxing completely against Gwen.

The dance should have been harmless, even platonic, Gwen thought. But she hadn't counted on having to look directly into Travis's eyes while they moved to the music. Cheek-to-cheek would have been one kind of sensual temptation, but gazing into those golden eyes seemed even more intimate.

He held her gaze, and even though his arms cradled her loosely, she felt cinched in tight by the warmth in his eyes. She couldn't glance away without seeming cowardly, or nervous, or lacking in confidence.

"You don't have to be afraid of me, Gwen," he said.

She lifted her chin. "I'm not."

In sleep, Elizabeth's hand slipped down and rested on the swell of Gwen's breast. The innocent touch ignited Gwen's already heated nerve endings.

Travis glanced down with a hint of a smile. Then his gaze moved back up and lingered on Gwen's mouth before returning to her eyes. There was a flicker of heat in the tawny depths that hadn't been there before. "Yeah, you're afraid," he said. "The pulse in your throat is going like sixties. But I won't hurt you."

She swallowed and tried to calm her breathing. Her senses filled with the scent of baby powder mingled with the spicy aroma of Travis's aftershave. A baby and a man to love—she hadn't realized how much she wanted that. Longing washed over her. "That's right, you won't hurt me, because I won't give you the chance."

"You know, there's a big difference between me and your ex."

"I don't want to talk about Derek."

"We won't. I have something to tell you about me."

She tried not to respond to the caressing tone in his voice. "I know all I need to know about you."

"I don't think so. Otherwise you wouldn't be afraid. Gwen, the only way people get hurt is when promises are broken. I won't do that."

She shivered at the way he spoke her name. "Because you don't make promises?"

"Not the forever kind." His fingers traced lazy patterns over her back. "But I can promise to make love to you honestly, thoroughly, and tenderly for whatever time we decide to spend together."

She didn't want him to know he was arousing her, but those eyes probably saw everything—her rapid breathing, her beating pulse, her flushed skin.

"If we both know what to expect going in, then nobody gets hurt," he murmured.

Oh, he was good. She wanted him to kiss her so much she could taste it. "I'll bet there are several women with broken hearts who wouldn't agree with your reasoning."

"Then they lied to themselves. I never lied to them."

His mouth was beautiful, she thought. Every woman should have a chance to kiss a mouth like that once in her life. And if the rest of him lived up to the sensuous promise of his mouth....

"You're thinking about it," he said. "That's a start."

"I'm thinking about what an arrogant man you are." Excitingly arrogant. She wondered if she was capable of lovemaking with no strings. Pleasure without promises. For the long run, it didn't fit into her dreams. But a forever man seemed like a distant and unreachable goal, and in the meantime she could allow herself to enjoy...no, it was too risky. But the fact that she was even wondering what it would be like to have an affair with Travis meant that he'd breached her defenses.

"I'm far from arrogant," he said, subtly caressing her back. "I can't afford to be when you have all the power."

"Ha. You're a world-class flirt, Travis. I can't even play in your league."

"You're selling yourself short. When I saw you come down the aisle of the church in that dynamite dress, my knees almost gave out. I'm a desperate man, Gwen, begging you to soften your heart."

She was getting soft, all right. Soft in the head, heart, everywhere. Outrageous though his compliments were, they were having an effect. Soon she'd be putty in his hands. "I don't want to be another notch on your belt," she said.

He smiled, slow and sexy, his eyes alight with banked passion. "Then let me be a notch in yours."

3

TRAVIS PRIDED HIMSELF on his ability to handle a room full of women and make each one of them feel special, but this reception was taxing his powers. And to be truthful, his heart wasn't in the effort. Flattering as it was to have all these ladies asking him to dance, he would have preferred a quiet little bar, a jukebox and Gwen in his arms.

He wasn't happy about the fact that she was out on the floor nearly as often as he was, and that she seemed to be having such a good time. Damn it, she wanted *him*. He'd seen it in her eyes when they'd shared that one frustrating dance, and he'd hoped for another dance with her once Elizabeth was tucked into the little bassinet Sebastian had set up in a corner. No telling where another dance might lead, considering the look in her eyes following the first one. He was eager to stoke the fire he'd started.

Instead he'd been besieged by the female population of Huerfano. He'd danced with nearly every woman in the room, and he'd been offered enough pieces of wedding cake to open his own bakery. Apparently his stint with Lizzie at the altar combined with his wedding toast had made him a very popular guy. Ordinarily he would have loved it, but tonight he was in a strange, one-woman kind of mood.

He was so busy that he barely had time to get himself a fresh beer. Finally he excused himself from Donna, the kindergarten teacher, and headed for the bar.

"Hey, Romeo." Sebastian caught his arm as he was heading back into the fray, a cold long-neck in one hand. "Got a minute?" He glanced at Travis's beer. "I'll buy you a drink."

Travis grinned, turned back to the bartender and lifted his bottle. "Get another one of these for the bridegroom, would you? The poor guy needs to live it up while he still has the chance."

"Yeah, I've got it tough," Sebastian said as he took the offered beer. "Not every guy could handle being married to a goddess, but fortunately I'm up to the job. Come on, let's get some air."

"I can see right off that my speech gave you a swelled head." Travis followed Sebastian outside. The air was cold, but it felt good after all the exercise he'd been getting on the dance floor. "Keep it up and I'll be obliged to round up a few guys to toss you in the horse trough."

"You think *I've* got a swelled head?" Sebastian leaned against the fender of the caterer's truck and unfastened the top button of his tux shirt. The string tie had been abandoned long ago. "After all the attention you've been getting tonight, it'll take three men and a boy to cram your hat on in the morning." He lifted his beer toward Travis and smiled. "Here's to one hell of a wedding."

Travis clinked his bottle to Sebastian's. "A great party for a great reason." He took a long swallow.

Sebastian sipped his beer and looked up at the night sky. "Full moon."

"I ordered it special."

Sebastian laughed. "Funny thing is, I believe you."

"Hey, I can do anything I set my mind to."

"Uh, huh. Evans, you really should work on that lack of confidence problem."

"I know what I know."

"Okay, you're amazing. But listen, I've been going over this honeymoon trip again, and I really think I ought to hire somebody to help you with Elizabeth while Matty and I are in Denver. We don't leave until noon, so I'm sure I could find somebody if I started calling around in the morning."

Travis stiffened. "You don't trust me with her."

"Sure I do. Well, maybe I didn't at first, but you've got the basics down. I'm worried about what you'll do if something goes wrong, though. We'd be at least three hours getting home, assuming we even got the message right away, and—"

"You are such an old granny, Daniels. I swear. I can handle it. If it's major I'll go to Doc Harrison. If it's minor, I'll go to Gwen." He'd just now thought of that, but the idea appealed to him. Not that he wanted any emergency to crop up concerning Lizzie. But the combination of him and the baby seemed to melt women's hearts. It might have a thawing effect on Gwen, too. Yeah, he just might have to consult Gwen on some baby-care question.

"What's up with you and Gwen, anyway?"

"What do you mean?" Travis took another swig of his beer, so he'd look cool and casual as he answered the question.

"I thought you two were like oil and water, but you were blending together pretty good during that dance earlier tonight."

"I think she's figured out I don't have horns and a forked tail, after all."

Sebastian gazed at him. "You do anything to hurt that woman, and Matty'll be the one with the pitchfork, aiming it straight at your sorry ass."

Travis blew out a breath. "Why does everybody think I'm out to break women's hearts?"

"It couldn't be on account of all the women you've left in tears, now could it?"

"Look, I've told each and every one of them I'm not in for the long haul. Is it my fault they won't listen?"

Sebastian took a drink of his beer and glanced up at the moon. "I told Matty I couldn't get serious, either, because of the baby and thinking I'd have to ask Jessica to marry me. That didn't stop Matty from getting hurt." He glanced back at Travis. "You can't order a woman not to fall in love with you."

Travis shifted uncomfortably under Sebastian's scrutiny. "I don't want Gwen to fall in love with me. I just—"

"Yeah, I know what you just. That dress she's wearing would make a monk leave his order."

Travis grinned. "Or revive a corpse at a wake."

Sebastian chuckled. "Or replace Viagra."

"I'm only human."

"I know all about your humanity," Sebastian said. "You're a legend in your own time. But go easy on this, okay? Gwen's a sweet lady and she had a rough few years with that husband of hers."

"I promise to be careful. We won't do anything that's not in our mutual best interests."

Sebastian nodded. "Good. And one other thing. If Jessica comes back while Matty and I are in Denver, you make her stay at the ranch until we can get home, okay?''

"Damn right I will. Jessica has some explaining to do, to all of us." And telling them who was Lizzie's father was the first thing, Travis thought. But he knew in his heart the little girl was his. Looks aside, Lizzie had his temperament. She was smart, easygoing and loved everybody.

"If I'm not convinced Jessica's in a position to take care of Elizabeth," Sebastian said, "I'm going to see what I can do about keeping the baby with us. I've checked into it, and abandoning your kid puts you on shaky legal ground."

Travis rubbed the back of his neck. "I still can't figure why she'd do that. It doesn't seem like the kind of thing the Jessica we know would even think of. Hell, it was her grit that saved Nat's life after the avalanche. Something pretty nasty must have scared the daylights out of her, to make her leave her kid like this."

"Yeah, and I want to find out what." Sebastian took another swig of his beer. "I've decided to hire a private investigator while we're in Denver."

"Good. I'll go halves with you on the fee. This is dragging out way too long."

"And it damned near made me lose Matty." Sebastian cocked an ear toward the tent. "And speaking of Matty, we'd better get back in. I think the bouquet and garter-throwing is about to start."

"Hey, you go ahead. I'd sooner catch a rattlesnake with my bare hands than that garter."

Sebastian laughed and shook his head. "I don't know what your problem is, Evans. You're twenty-eight, for crying out loud. The carefree single life must be getting old by now."

"Nah. It's terrific."

"So's marriage. Or at least I plan on it being terrific, this time around."

"For you, maybe. Not for this cowboy." Travis tipped the bottle back for a deep swallow of beer.

"Well, you gotta come back in and pretend to try for the garter. You're the best man, which means you should act like you're part of the proceedings. It'll look bad if you're not there."

"I'll be in shortly." Travis lifted his bottle. "And thanks for the beer."

"It'll come out of your paycheck. Don't forget—now that Matty and I are combining our spreads, you'll be working for me."

Travis clutched his chest and staggered backward in mock horror. "Don't tell me I have to start calling you *boss?*"

"Or Your Royal Highness. Whichever comes easier."

"How about Your Royal Pain in the Ass?" Travis grinned. "That comes real easy."

Sebastian rolled his eyes. "When I throw the garter, I'm aiming for you, hotshot. You need a woman to trim your wick. Now get your butt in there."

"Shortly."

"Insubordination already." Sebastian sighed and went back inside the tent.

Travis figured he'd stall around outside and appear at the tail end of the garter-throwing. He wasn't overly superstitious, but a guy couldn't be too careful.

He'd thought about marriage, more than he'd ever admit to Sebastian, and he'd reasoned out that it was too complicated given his present circumstances. A promise was a promise, and he'd made a huge one to his dad before the old man died six years ago. Travis intended to honor that promise and take care of his mother, who depended on him something fierce.

She managed okay during the summer months, when she could walk to the little country store down the road from their place. In the winter, though, when the snow was up to her armpits, she needed Travis there to shovel the walkways and drive her where she had to go.

No one in this valley knew anything about his life in Utah, and that's the way he liked it. If folks around here thought he was a devil-may-care playboy, that was fine with him. But the truth was that keeping his mother healthy and happy took all of his resources. He couldn't imagine having enough energy left for a wife.

GWEN HADN'T PLANNED to take part in the bouquet tossing, but Matty had informed her it was obligatory. So she moved to the back of the crowd of women, figuring Matty wouldn't heave the thing that far.

As the women stood there laughing and joking, Matty turned her back and sent the flowers sailing...right over everybody's head. Gwen was forced to leap up and snag it or the beautiful bouquet would have landed on the floor. For a split second she considered letting that happen, but that would have created an awkward moment. With skills learned on the volleyball court as a kid, she pulled down the prize.

Everybody in the room cheered, and Gwen stood there holding the bouquet and feeling like a doofus. She was immensely grateful when the attention returned to Matty for the garter removal ceremony.

Amid a chorus of wolf whistles, Matty propped one foot on a chair and pulled back her skirt.

Sebastian quickly and efficiently divested her of the garter. Twirling it neatly around one finger, he turned toward the circle of men. "Show's over, gents. And let that be the last whistle I hear any of you aim in my wife's direction. *Comprende?*"

"Killjoy!" called out one of the cowboys.

"No, *husband*," Sebastian replied with a dangerous-looking smile. "Now, where the hell's Evans?"

Gwen glanced around and realized that Travis hadn't come back in with Sebastian. She'd seen the two men head outside. Embarrassingly enough, she'd been aware of every move Travis had made that night. None of them had been in her direction.

"Evans?" one of the men said with a laugh. "You'll never get that ol' boy within twenty feet of a wedding garter. Toss that thing my way, Daniels. I could use another dance with the Maid of Honor."

"Not if I get to that lace thingamajig first," said the cowboy next to him.

"You'll have to get past me," said a third man.

Gratifying as it was to have men squabbling over the right to dance with her, Gwen couldn't work up a smidgen of enthusiasm for any of them. And damn, but she wished she could. They were nice guys, steady guys.

Apparently she hadn't meditated enough on the dangers of being attracted to a rogue. The only man in the vicinity who held her interest was the last man she should spend time with. Fortunately he was still out-side and wasn't in the running for the garter.

"I guess we'll have to do this without Evans," Sebastian said. "And watch those elbows. I'd like to think we're all gentlemen here," he added with a grin.

"I'd like to think so, too, but I don't," said the first cowboy. "And that garter's mine."

"May the best man win." Sebastian aimed the garter into the air like a slingshot.

"Somebody called?" Travis stepped into the tent.

"Now that's cutting it close," Sebastian muttered as he let the garter fly.

Gwen knew Travis had amazing reflexes. He could rope and tie a calf faster than anybody in the valley, and he wasn't shy about saying so. But the lightning moves he demonstrated as he snatched the garter out of the air left the women gasping and the men swearing.

"What'd you do that for?" complained Jason Litchfield, a lanky cowhand who'd been hitting on Gwen all night. "Everybody knows you're not lookin' to get tied down, and catching that thing means you'll be the next one hitched."

Travis shrugged and tucked the garter in his pocket as he started toward Gwen. "Maybe, maybe not. But I've been wanting to dance with the maid of honor all night, and you boys have been keeping her so busy, I haven't been able to get close."

Gwen stood frozen in place, her heart beating like a rabbit's. There would be no baby between them this time.

Just before Travis reached her, Sebastian came over and clapped him on the back. "Congratulations on catching that garter. It would do my heart good to see you finally settle down with the right woman."

Travis glanced at him. "It'll take more than a garter to get me to the altar, buddy."

"Oh, I'm sure it will." Sebastian winked at Gwen. "But it's a start. Now if you'll excuse me, I'm going to find the previous owner of that garter and take her for a turn around the floor."

Travis gazed at Gwen. Then he swept out an arm and bowed. "May I have this dance?"

"I guess so." She put her hand in his and allowed him to lead her to the dance floor. Just the casual interlacing of their fingers quickened her breath. "You worked hard enough for it."

"Piece of cake. Hand-eye coordination has always been easy for me."

"And you're so modest about it, too."

He chuckled and swung her into his arms.

She rested the hand holding the bridal bouquet on his shoulder, and with every swirl of the waltz step, the fragrance of roses and lavender drifted around them, toying with her senses. She'd expected an aggressively sexual man like Travis to pull her in close and get all the body contact he could manage. Instead he kept several inches between them, guiding her with a firm hand at her waist while cupping her right hand gently, yet expertly, in his.

But once again, he held her captive with his gaze. And Travis could do more with his eyes than any man she'd ever met. She'd danced with many partners tonight, and all of them had pulled her in tight, blatantly announcing their sexual interest with their bodies. Not one of them had made her sizzle.

She was sizzling now. The spot where Travis pressed the small of her back became an erogenous zone, sending arousing signals to every part of her body. His eyes seduced her, inviting her to imagine making love with him. His rhythmic skill on the dance floor hinted at his legendary skill in the bedroom.

She'd heard the whispered rumors about Travis, and her imagination filled in the rest. She guessed that he was the kind of lover women dreamed of in their deepest, most erotic moments. The kind even *she* had dreamed of, but never planned to have.

Because he was dangerous. He could break her heart so that it would never heal. And yet...he could make her secret fantasies come true, teach her things about her own sensuality that no other man could. But he would not stay. He would never stay.

The silence between them became heavy with unspoken desire. She struggled to break the spell. "I'm amazed you went for the garter," she said. "I guess you're not superstitious."

"I am sort of superstitious." His grip at her waist tightened a fraction. "But this looked like the only way I was going to get another dance with you. I decided it might be worth tempting fate."

She swallowed. "And is it?"

"Oh, I think it will be." His glance swept her face, slid down her throat, settled for a second longer than was polite on her breasts. Then he returned his gaze to her eyes. Hunger flickered there as he drew her a bare inch closer, so that the bodice of her dress brushed the front of his tux shirt, catching lightly on the pearl studs with each movement.

The contact was faint, subtle. Yet her nipples tightened and her breathing grew labored.

"Is that bed and breakfast of yours full?" he murmured.

"Why?" She had to keep her head. "Are you angling for personal service?"

"Nope." He drew her in a little bit more, causing her sensitive breasts to be crushed gently against the hard wall of his chest. "Just wondered how business was."

She could feel his heartbeat, rapid like hers. She should push away from him, but couldn't make herself do it. For the first time in months, maybe years, she felt alive again. "Business is a little slow right now." She cleared the hoarseness from her throat. "The skiers are gone, and the summer season doesn't usually get going until after Memorial Day."

"Hmm." Neatly, without fanfare, he broke eye contact, snugged her up close and laid his cheek against hers. "So what do you do with yourself all day?"

She closed her eyes against the wash of passion that left her shaking. "I weave," she whispered. With each movement they made, she felt the nudge of his erection. Her body moistened, pulsed, yearned.

His lips touched her ear. "I like the blanket you made Lizzie. It's so soft."

"Mmm." Oh, she ached as she'd never ached in her life.

His voice was like velvet. "Say yes, Gwen. Say yes and let me love you."

Her heart thundered in her chest. She didn't hear the music stop.

But Travis obviously had, because he slowly released her and drew back to look deeply into her eyes. Heat burned in his gaze, and his hands at her waist quivered with urgency. "Please say yes," he whispered. "I need you."

She couldn't speak. His obvious desire called out to

her, teasing her with the promise of fantasies fulfilled, begging her to forget everything else and be swept away by shared passion. Calling upon the last scrap of sanity left in her fevered brain, she shook her head.

4

TRAVIS DIDN'T TAKE Gwen's rejection personally. And because he was an expert at reading women, he didn't even believe it. Other guys might get themselves into trouble with no-means-yes situations and either miss an opportunity or, worse yet, force the issue and get slapped.

Travis had never missed an opportunity, and he'd never been slapped. He'd been told by some of his drinking buddies that he should give a clinic on how to understand a lady, no matter what words came out of her pretty mouth.

The secret could be summed up in two words—body language. When he'd propositioned Gwen, and he'd done a damn fine job of it, too, she'd shaken her head no. But he'd be a fool to accept that.

At the same time she was shaking her head, her skin was flushed and hot, her pupils were dilated, her mouth was parted and her breathing was uneven. She was leaning so far toward him that she was in danger of toppling over. Or into his arms. Gwen might think she was saying no with that shake of her head, but the rest of her was screaming yes.

But now was not the time to touch her. Now was not the time to challenge her decision, either.

"Okay," he murmured. "I'll respect that."

Her eyes widened. "You will?" Disappointment was written all over her face.

He bit his tongue to keep from laughing. "Of course. What sort of a jerk do you think I am? I gave it my best shot and you're still not interested. I'm not about to make a fool out of myself."

She straightened and moved back a pace. "Uh, that's good. Because you would have if you'd kept insisting." She rubbed a hand over the soft green material stretched across her rib cage, as if calming butterflies in her stomach. "It's good we got that settled."

He nodded, taking note of the pulse beating rapidly at the base of her throat. "Right. I like to know where I stand."

Longing shone in her eyes, but she glanced away. "Well, now you do." She gave him one more quick look. "I'd better check with Matty and see if she needs anything."

"You do that."

"Travis!" a woman called from across the room. "The next dance is mine!"

Travis turned, recognizing Donna's voice. "Absolutely!" he called out in reply. When he turned back, Gwen was gone.

ABOUT AN HOUR later Gwen lined up with the rest of the guests to pelt Matty and Sebastian with birdseed while the newlyweds made their way over to the ranch house. She headed up a line on one side of the tent entrance and Travis stood across from her in the other line.

Resisting Travis had been for the best, Gwen told herself. She just wished he hadn't given up so quickly. And he definitely seemed to have given up. He'd spent the past hour dancing and flirting with his many admirers, not that she'd noticed, or anything. Ha. Her jaw ached from gritting her teeth.

She watched him joking with Donna, who seemed to have the inside track at the moment. Gwen had to admit that Travis's pursuit this evening had been one of the more exciting episodes in her life.

Maybe *the* most exciting episode, now that she thought about it. She didn't exactly lead a thrill-packed life. The word *dull* came to mind. But she hadn't been able to figure out how to have both stability and excitement, so she'd chosen stability.

Travis had offered her a chance for a little excitement, and chicken that she was, she'd refused him. Deep down, she was afraid she wasn't wild enough for Travis. He'd probably tire of her quickly, and then he'd be the one to call it quits. Like Derek. How embarrassing.

If she could simply enjoy his attentions and then cut off the relationship before he did, she might have considered his offer. But she'd hung on to Derek way too long, and she could easily make the same mistake with Travis. Besides, Travis was no longer extending his offer, so debating the issue in her head was stupid and unproductive.

"Here they come!" yelled Travis. "Man your birdseed!"

Gwen poured the contents of her little packet into her hand. Matty and Sebastian, carrying a blanket-covered Elizabeth, emerged from the tent into the light of the full moon. As they hurried through the gauntlet amid cheers and shouts, Gwen tossed the birdseed into the air and silently wished them all the babies they wanted.

And she would play the role of Auntie Gwen. She would weave blankets for each one, she thought, and offer to baby-sit, and bake them cinnamon rolls. Maybe it was better to spoil someone else's children instead of having the constant hassle of having your own. Maybe. But she didn't really think so.

Once Matty, Sebastian and the baby were inside the ranch house, the guests began their round of good-byes. Following Matty's instructions, Gwen gave away the centerpieces and any extra favors. As she moved through the departing crowd, she noticed that several women besides Donna hung around Travis, as if hoping he might pick one to take home with him. Not wanting to know whether he did or not, she went back into the tent to help the caterers pack up and make sure nobody had left any belongings behind.

Finally the caterers removed all the coffee urns and bagged up all the table linens. At the last moment Gwen snatched up Matty's bridal bouquet so it wouldn't accidentally be tossed in one of the large plastic garbage bags by mistake.

As she listened to the catering truck pull away, she gazed around the silent, empty tent and sighed. Nothing more to do except throw the switch on the small white lights and go home. The party, as they said, was over.

"You look tired."

Gwen whirled to find Travis walking toward her. A night of partying had left him looking appealingly disheveled, and the glow from the tiny white lights overhead added a roguish sparkle to his gaze. But he'd said he'd respect her wishes, so he wasn't here to try and seduce her.

Her heart began to pound anyway. "I thought everyone had left by now."

"Everyone but me. I thought I'd better stay and find out if there's anything more to do."

"That's nice of you, but I think we're fine." She should get the hell out of here while the getting was good. "All that's left is turning out the lights." She stroked the rose petals of the bouquet, needing something to do with her hands. "The rental company will come out tomorrow to pick up the tables and chairs and the tent."

He nodded and glanced around at the bare tables. "It looked pretty."

"It really did." Being alone with him was starting to have an effect, making her tremble. She clutched the bouquet more tightly. "Listen, I probably should go—"

"Yeah, me, too. So that's it? You're sure there's nothing else?"

She didn't know how he'd managed to get so close to her, but before she realized it, he was near enough that she could see the gold flecks in his warm brown eyes. And if that wasn't a seductive look he was giving her, she'd never seen one before.

Her pulse raced. "Nothing else. It went like clockwork."

"Yeah, it did. But I have a nagging feeling we forgot something." His beautiful mouth curved in a soft smile.

That mouth. That talented mouth. She wanted to know what his kiss would be like. And he saw through her. She was sure of it. He knew that right this minute, she was imagining the way his lips would taste.

"You know that feeling?" he said. "That you've missed some detail?"

She struggled to take a breath. "I don't have that feeling."

"I do," he murmured. His gaze drifted to the bouquet she held like a shield between them. He stroked a rosebud, loosening the pink petals with deft fingers. Then he plucked one free and lifted it to her mouth, slowly brushing it over her bottom lip.

She grew dizzy. "Go away, Travis," she whispered.

"Can't, Gwen." The rose petal fluttered to the ground as he cupped her jaw, holding her steady as he lowered his head. "I just remembered what I forgot."

She could still escape, she thought wildly as his breath drifted warm and sweet across her mouth. She could still pull back and run away, still save herself if she just....

Too late. Ahhh...way too late. Way too good. The mouth of an angel...the tongue of a devil. Oh, *yes*.

Later she might regret this moment, but no woman could think of regret when a man was kissing her like this. He was delicious, tasting of wine and wedding cake and the wild, heady flavor of desire. And he knew what he was doing. Oh boy, did he know. Everyone had a special talent, and it seemed she'd just discovered his. She wrapped greedy arms around him and pulled him close, body to heated body, while his mouth worked magic on hers.

His kiss became a messenger, sending urgent signals to her breasts, her inner thighs, her throbbing womb. She grew taut, moist, ready. Resistance was a dim memory eclipsed by the glowing prospect of surrender.

He lifted his lips a fraction from hers. "Come home with me."

Yes. She gasped for air so that she could give him an answer, the only possible answer now that he'd kissed her so thoroughly and left her body thrumming with need.

"Hey, is anybody still here?"

Travis released her immediately and they both turned as Sebastian walked into the tent.

Gwen's cheeks warmed. She put more distance between her and Travis and clutched the bouquet in both hands to disguise how she was shaking.

Sebastian took one look at them and backed up a couple of steps. "Whoops. Sorry. We saw the lights were still on and Matty asked me to come out and check on the situation. Sorry."

Travis cleared his throat. "We'll, uh, make sure the lights are out when we leave."

"I knew that," Sebastian said, backing up into the shadows outside the tent.

"Didn't suppose you'd be taking time to glance out the window on your wedding night," Travis said.

His comment blew like a cool breeze through Gwen's fevered brain. Matty and Sebastian were enjoying a wedding night, but all Travis had offered was an affair. That just wasn't good enough.

"Elizabeth woke up and started fussing," Sebastian said. "Listen, I'll just go on back, okay? Travis, I'll see you up at the house about eleven in the morning."

"I'll be there."

"See you then. Sorry for the interruption."

Gwen took a deep breath. "I'll be going now, too, Sebastian. Maybe you'd be willing to walk me to my truck." She headed for the entrance with a determined step.

"Sure," Sebastian said. "But—"

"I'm sure Travis knows how to shut off the lights."

"I do," Travis said, "but I was hoping—"

"It's been a long evening." She glanced over her shoulder at him and forced herself to ignore the hard tug of sexual desire. "Good night, Travis."

His gaze was hot enough to melt steel. "Good night, Gwen."

He was darned potent. If Sebastian hadn't been there, she might have forgotten her principles and run back into his arms. But Sebastian's presence reminded her of what she really wanted from a man—forever. Tempting as he was, Travis didn't fill the bill.

THE FOLLOWING NIGHT Travis sank into Sebastian's old pine rocker and leaned his head back in complete exhaustion. Fleafarm, Sebastian's mixed breed, and Sadie, Matty's Great Dane, plopped at his feet.

Travis didn't remember being this tired even after a day of branding. Babies were a hell of a lot of work, but there were compensations. Lizzie was a smart little dickens. In no time at all, he'd taught her to blow an outstanding raspberry.

Her new trick had been kind of a liability when he'd tried to feed her cereal tonight, but they'd had fun playing with the stuff. He'd let her paint his face with it until he looked like some undead character from a horror flick.

Then she'd needed a bath, and some time to play on the baby gym he'd bought her last week. And finally he'd given her a bottle, changed her diaper again, and tucked her into bed. She was asleep at last, and Travis wondered if he had enough energy left to fix himself a sandwich.

As he contemplated whether he'd take the time to eat or give up and crawl into bed, he thought about Gwen. He'd fully intended to do a quick follow-up with her this afternoon after he was settled into his baby-sitting routine. He'd figured he and Lizzie would pay a little afternoon social call to Hawthorne House and see if they could get invited for dinner.

His plan had fizzled. He'd spent the time Lizzie was sleeping running a load of baby clothes through the washer and dryer, and by the time she woke up from her nap it was time to check on the horses, feed the dogs, and feed Lizzie. Thank God Matty had moved her saddle horses up to the Rocking D, or he'd have run himself ragged going back and forth between her barn and Sebastian's.

But it would be a busier week than he'd thought, that was for sure. Unfortunately, the longer he went without seeing Gwen, the more likely she'd go cold on him again. He'd had her warmed up pretty good last night, and he'd been in a state of semi-arousal ever since. He'd welcome some relief for that condition, but he wouldn't be getting it tonight.

Doggone Sebastian's hide, anyway. But you couldn't land into a guy right before his honeymoon, so Travis hadn't even had the satisfaction of yelling at Sebastian for ruining the moment. Besides, Travis wasn't convinced it had been an accident. Matty didn't want him getting involved with Gwen. If she'd noticed his truck and Gwen's still parked by the tent, she might have sent Sebastian out on purpose.

Travis sighed. Kissing Gwen had turned out to be better than he'd expected. She'd reminded him of what kissing had been like when he'd first discovered it and had been totally fascinated with the pleasure of exploring a girl's mouth. Later on in his education, he'd progressed to other areas of a woman's anatomy, and he'd been guilty of downgrading kissing to a preliminary step leading to more interesting activities.

With Gwen he could imagine kissing as an end in itself. Or at least something to pass the time for a good long while. Her mouth was soft and supple, full in a way that made him want to nibble, welcoming in a way that made him want to thrust deep with his tongue. She tasted sweet and spicy, which was the way he'd imagine she'd be in bed.

The crotch of his jeans grew tight. Apparently he wasn't as exhausted as he'd thought. He'd better think of something else besides taking Gwen to bed if he wanted to sleep tonight. He wondered if she was frustrated too. She might be, but he doubted she'd show her hand enough to drive over here tonight, even if he called and asked her to.

Still, it was a thought. He could say he wanted her to check out something to do with Lizzie. No, that would be too underhanded. He was doing fine with Lizzie.

He could be bold and say he couldn't stop thinking about her, which was true. Maybe, if he explained that he was stuck here, she'd take pity on him and consider—

The ringing phone sent adrenaline pumping through him. The dogs leaped up, too, and the three of them hurried to the kitchen. Travis grabbed the cordless receiver from its cradle, hoping that his prayers were about to be answered. "Hello?" He sounded too eager, but he couldn't help that. He was eager.

"Who is this?"

He paused. The caller was a woman, but it definitely wasn't Gwen. He went on alert. "That depends on who you are."

"Jessica."

He should have known. Sebastian had warned him she often called late at night.

"It's Travis, Jessica." He headed for Sebastian's office, where the tracing equipment was set up. "Listen, you need to get back here. Whatever you're afraid of—"

"I can't be near Elizabeth. It's not safe for her. Is she okay?"

"She's fine. But I deserve to know if I'm her—"

Click.

Travis clenched the receiver and swore softly. So much for tracing the call. Even if he'd been prepared to do it, she hadn't stayed on the line long enough. And even if she had, he wasn't in a position to go tearing off in search of her. She could be hundreds of miles away. And once she'd made the call, she'd probably leave the area, anyway. That's what he'd do if he didn't want to be found.

He returned to the kitchen and hung up the phone. In the process he glanced at the list of numbers tacked to the small bulletin board Matty had hung on the wall. She'd made several small changes like that in the past couple of weeks, putting her stamp on Sebastian's house. Her floor loom now occupied a corner of the living room, and one of her favorite paintings of a mare and foal hung over the fireplace.

She'd directed Travis's attention to the list of phone numbers at least four times before she and Sebastian had left for Denver that morning. Doc Harrison had top billing and was in red, no less. Next came the vet. Then relatives. Then Gwen.

Travis stared at Gwen's number for several long seconds. After all, he did have news. Jessica had called again.

He picked up the receiver and punched in Gwen's number. It rang twice before he thought to glance at the clock, and by then it was too late. He'd already disturbed her at an ungodly hour.

"Hawthorne House." She didn't sound the least bit sleepy.

"It's Travis." He wondered if she was still awake because she was frustrated and edgy, too. He hoped so.

"Is the baby okay?" she asked quickly.

"She's perfect. I just got a call from Jessica."

"You did?" Excitement laced her response. "Did she say anything new?"

"Only that it wasn't safe for her to be around Lizzie. But we'd kind of figured that."

"So she didn't say..."

"Who fathered Lizzie? Nope. But I guess it doesn't matter. I know she's mine."

"You sound proud of the fact."

He thought about that. "I guess I am," he said with some surprise. "I know it shouldn't have happened in the first place, but now that Lizzie's here, I'm not sorry. I'm gonna spend as much time as possible with her while she's growing up."

"Imagine that. Travis Evans making a commitment to a female."

She was getting snippy, he thought. His idea of inviting her over might be a pipe dream. "I make commitments to women all the time."

"Sure you do."

"If I'm involved with a woman, she's the only one in my life during that time. That's a commitment."

"Pardon me if I'm underwhelmed by such virtue."

He wished he had her right in front of him instead of on the telephone. Talking wasn't getting them anywhere. Action was what they both needed. "Not everybody is cut out for marriage. At least I'm honest about that."

"Okay, then let me be equally honest with you. Get lost."

He'd decided that her sass was a defense against her strong feelings for him. "Then I guess you aren't planning to drop by tonight to keep me company."

"In your dreams."

"Oh, you'll be in my dreams, all right. Last night you were the main feature."

"Funny, but I didn't dream at all last night." She sounded like the damned Queen of England.

He was beginning to like that snooty attitude of hers. It would make her surrender that much sweeter. "Of course you didn't dream. You were wide awake and frustrated, wishing I was there."

"Travis, your ego is huge!"

He grinned. "True, but women tell me it matches my...personality."

"I'm hanging up this phone."

"Good. Hang up and drive over. You sound tense. Let me give you a massage. I use the heel of my hand on the big muscles, and my fingers for some of the smaller ones. And there's a spot on your inner thigh that—"

A gentle click on the other end of the line told him she'd hung up. He wished he could believe she was on her way to the Rocking D, but he doubted it. He'd have to go to her, and with the way Lizzie kept him hopping, that would be more difficult than he'd thought.

5

GWEN TOOK OFF the tea towel she'd draped over the mixing bowl sitting on her kitchen counter. Then she punched her fist into the swollen mound of dough inside. It was the most satisfaction she'd had all day.

Dressed in her favorite at-home outfit of soft, faded sweats, her hair caught in a casual topknot, she was consoling herself by making comfort food—her famous cinnamon rolls.

And she definitely needed comfort this afternoon. After Travis's provocative phone call two nights ago, he'd dropped out of sight. She wished he'd dropped out of mind, too, but no such luck. In addition to battling frustration over Travis, she'd had to deal with the latest e-mail from her mother, who was currently on a dig near Cairo.

Her mother had wanted to know when Gwen was planning to stop "playing house" and continue her academic career. Gwen was the only member of the family without a college degree and an intellectual job, and that had bothered her mother for years.

After sprinkling flour on the butcher-block surface, Gwen scooped the dough out and began kneading it with firm, vigorous strokes. She was good at this, damn it. It might not be rocket science, but she took satisfaction in turning out a cinnamon roll that made her guests groan with delight.

Her mother might be able to identify a pre-Columbian artifact at a thousand paces, but when she'd tackled baking from scratch, her yeast had died and her cinnamon rolls had been hard as hockey pucks. She'd pronounced the whole exercise not worth her time in the first place, claiming that people ate too much of that stuff anyway.

Intellectually, Gwen had known that her mother dissed baking because she couldn't do it. Her mother had laughingly called Gwen a throwback who for some strange reason excelled at anything domestic. The subtle put-down might have salvaged her mother's ego, but it hadn't done much for Gwen's.

This morning's e-mail probably bothered her more because she wasn't sleeping well. She tried to blame her insomnia on not having enough to do now that Matty and Sebastian's wedding was over. No guests were due until the following weekend, and she didn't dare plant her seedlings in the garden until the frost warnings were over for the season. Her weaving, which had never failed to calm her, was failing her now. She needed the big muscle movement of cleaning up after guests, planting veggies or...or having sex.

Well, *that* wouldn't be happening, so she might as well get her sensory kicks out of kneading dough. And it was sensual, she admitted as she pushed the heel of her hand into the soft, yielding surface. On the phone the other night Travis had said he used the heel of his hand on the big muscles, and his fingers on the smaller ones....

And just like that, her mind leaped back inside the squirrel cage. It spun around chasing the subject of Travis while her hands followed the familiar steps of making cinnamon rolls. The action of the marble rolling pin flattening the dough reminded her of the way Travis had stroked her back while they danced. She remembered the silkiness of his kiss when she slid a knife into a stick of softened butter and spread the butter over the dough.

Butter was a more erotic substance than she'd realized, and she grew fascinated with the creamy slide of it as she moved the knife blade over the pliable surface of the dough. She wondered how butter would feel on her skin, how it would feel to have someone lick it off.

A certain someone.

The scent of sugar and cinnamon reminded her of Travis's aftershave. She sprinkled raisins over the surface of the buttered dough and rolled it into a cylinder—a cylinder that fit her hand with the same thickness and heft as...oh, dear. She was hopeless.

She blew out an impatient breath and sliced the cylinder deliberately into sections. Fate had played a cruel trick on her, giving her a talent for creating a hearth and home, then making her susceptible to rogues who never intended to settle down.

She'd thought Derek had cured her of her weakness for a knowing wink and a sexy smile. After suffering through the insensitive behavior of her husband, she should run in the opposite direction when a man tried his devilish ways on her. Yet here she was, longing for another bad boy as if she hadn't learned a single thing during her marriage.

Travis would never know how close she'd come to driving out to the Rocking D the night he'd called. Good thing she hadn't, because his silence for the past two days indicated that he'd lost interest already. Maybe he didn't have time to fool with someone who didn't fall immediately into his clutches. Maybe he'd moved on to Donna, who would have driven out to the ranch before Travis had time to hang up the phone.

The doorbell rang as she put the rolls in the oven. Telling herself to expect the mailman or a solicitor, she deliberately took her time rinsing the flour off her hands and wiping them dry before walking down the hall toward the front door. The door's oval stained-glass insert gave her an indistinct picture of the person on the other side, but her heart recognized Travis and the baby immediately. Her pulse kicked into high gear.

She paused to take a deep breath and tamp down her eagerness. Travis was difficult enough to manage when he wasn't quite sure of himself. If he suspected she'd been thinking of him for two solid days, the situation would be out of control in no time. No doubt he'd brought the baby over as a ploy to soften her resistance. Little did he know he didn't need the baby to make Gwen as pliable as the dough she'd just been shaping.

But she straightened her spine and reminded herself he hadn't contacted her for two days. And for the time being, she still had her pride.

Turning the polished brass knob, she opened the door and promptly forgot all her resolutions as compassion swept over her. A cool spring breeze blew across the porch, and Travis had wrapped Elizabeth in a light blanket as he cradled her against his chest. She was fussing, and he looked completely done in.

"Lizzie has caught a cold," he said. "If you don't want to expose yourself to her germs, that's okay, but—"

"Come in." Gwen stepped back from the door and held out her arms. "And let me have that poor baby."

Travis looked as if she'd offered him a million dollars. "Thanks, Gwen. You don't know how much this means to me." He settled the squirming baby in her arms. "I've just been to Doc Harrison's for a diagnosis and Coogan's Department Store for supplies. The doc says it's nothing to worry about, but I'm fit to be tied."

"Poor Elizabeth," Gwen crooned as she unwrapped the baby and noticed that her button nose was red and her usually bright eyes dull. "I'll bet she picked up something at the wedding."

Travis closed the door. "That's what the doc says. He told me not to worry, that babies catch colds all the time, but I purely hate this."

"Of course you do." Gwen noticed Elizabeth's nose was running. "Come on back to the kitchen. I'll get a tissue." She hurried down the hall and ducked into the downstairs bathroom to grab a tissue from the wicker dispenser on the vanity. "Poor sweetie," she murmured, wiping the tiny nose gently as she continued on into the kitchen.

Travis stood in the middle of the room looking endearingly unsure of himself. And damned sexy. He wore old jeans with the same flair as he wore a tuxedo.

But he was nervous. She could tell by the way he took off his Stetson and ran his fingers through his hair before clamping his hat on his head again. Travis wasn't the sort to fool with his clothes. He was usually too busy being swashbuckling.

Today he didn't seem the least interested in charming her. All his attention was focused on the baby. "Do you think we should call Matty and Sebastian?" he asked. "Doc said it's not necessary, but I think maybe—"

"Let's not," Gwen said. "We'd probably scare them to death, and she'll no doubt be all better by the time they get home, anyway."

Elizabeth began to fret.

Gwen jiggled her and wiped her nose again. "Poor darling. It's not fun having a stuffy nose, is it?" She glanced up at Travis. "Did you bring her bottle with you?"

"Yeah. Her diaper bag's out in the truck, but it's hard to get her to drink when her nose is clogged up. I bought apple juice because the doc thought I should give her some, and Nellie Coogan sold me this thingamajig that looks like a tiny turkey baster. Nellie said you use it to suck the stuff out of her nose, but I'd be scared spitless to use it on her. I bought a small jar of Vaseline for her sore nose, and a humidifier. And one of those Barney guys."

Gwen blinked. "I was with you all the way until you got to Barney."

"He's that dinosaur on TV. Kids go wild for him."

"I know that much." Gwen rocked Elizabeth, trying to distract the baby from her discomfort. "I have kids staying here at Hawthorne House sometimes. But what does Barney have to do with getting over a cold?"

"When you're sick, you need a poor-me present," he said with the first show of confidence he'd displayed since he'd appeared on her doorstep. "Everybody knows that."

"Oh." Gwen held back a smile. "Of course."

Travis glanced at Elizabeth, who was making pitiful little noises of unhappiness. "So you really don't think

we should call Matty and Sebastian? They called last
night and I told them everything was fine. Then this
morning Lizzie was all stuffed up. Maybe they'd want
to know."

Gwen thought of how excited Matty had been while
she planned for her week in the big city. She and
Gwen had shopped for days buying slinky dresses for
nights out on the town, and revealing negligees for
private moments in the honeymoon suite of one of
Denver's finest hotels. Matty had never been treated
to such luxury.

"I hate to tell them," Gwen said. "This is a special
time for both of them, and if Doc Harrison said Elizabeth's not in any danger, it seems a shame to get them
upset. They might even think they should come home.
And I honestly don't think having them home would
make a bit of difference. This will just have to run its
course."

"But what if she gets worse? The doc didn't rule
that out."

"Well, then you can call them, I guess. But I think
calling them now is premature."

Travis stuck his hands in his hip pockets and blew
out a breath. Then he glanced at her. "Okay, I'll accept
that. But I'm scared to take her back out to the ranch
and be there alone with her. It's a good twenty minute
drive to town, and if she suddenly got bad, I'd—"

"You want to leave her here with me, don't you?"
Gwen discovered she wouldn't mind in the least. In
fact, she'd welcome the chance to have Elizabeth, even
if she did have a cold. In the years of running the bed
and breakfast, Gwen had encountered her share of
sick babies, and the prospect of taking care of Eliza-

beth while she was under the weather didn't worry her nearly as much as it obviously did Travis.

"Not exactly." Travis looked her straight in the eye. "This is going to sound suspicious to you, all things considered. But I swear I don't mean anything underhanded by it. I'm caught in the middle here. I'm afraid to be out on the Rocking D alone with Lizzie, so far from town and Doc Harrison, but I don't think I could stand leaving her with you overnight, either. I want to be with her, in case she gets worse."

Reaction shivered up Gwen's spine. He'd never looked at her like that, with no twinkle in his golden eyes, no hidden agenda lurking behind his steady gaze. She couldn't doubt his sincerity or his deep concern for the baby, and yet…how could she possibly invite him to stay here? And how could she not?

"I wouldn't blame you for turning me down," Travis said. "But I don't know what else to do."

"You could have taken her to Donna's," Gwen said quietly. "After all, she's a kindergarten teacher."

He shook his head. "Donna doesn't know Lizzie like you do. She only saw her for the first time at the wedding. And Matty's not all that fond of Donna, to be honest. Thinks she's overbearing and pushy. Matty would expect me to ask for your help, not Donna's. As far as Matty's concerned, you're practically family."

Gwen wiped Elizabeth's nose again and kissed the top of her head. She did feel connected to this little girl, which probably wasn't wise, considering the baby wouldn't ever be Gwen's, in any sense of the word. "That's nice to hear."

"I don't know if you'll believe me, but I promise to behave myself. All I care about is getting Lizzie well and staying close to the doctor in case she needs something."

Gwen looked into his eyes. In times past, he'd made her heart flutter with his rakish glances, but he'd never stirred her so deeply as now, when the only emotion she saw was loving concern for the baby he believed to be his. Perhaps she'd been hasty in judging him as superficial. In his worry over Elizabeth, he seemed to have completely forgotten his sexual needs.

"You can both stay." She mentally crossed her fingers and hoped she'd be strong enough to weather this. "It does seem like the best way to make sure Elizabeth will be safe and well."

His shoulders sagged in relief. "I don't know what I would have done if you'd said no."

"I'm doing this for Lizzie, and for Matty and Sebastian."

A ghost of a grin crossed his handsome face. "Oh, I don't doubt that. Without Lizzie, I probably wouldn't have made it past your front door today."

"True enough." And she wanted him to keep right on believing that. "Maybe you'd better bring in her diaper bag and all the things you bought."

"Yeah." He started out of the kitchen and paused. "You said you sometimes have kids here. Do you have a crib around?"

"I do. But what about your chores at the ranch? Is everything all right out there for the next twenty-four hours?"

He looked stricken. "My God, you're right. I forgot about the dogs and the horses. I can't believe I did that. I'd...I'd appreciate it if you wouldn't let Matty and Sebastian know that I forgot about the animals."

"You've been worried, and I'm sure they'd want

your top priority to be Elizabeth." She was touched that he'd been so preoccupied with the baby. And there was no doubt in her mind that he hadn't planned this overnight stay. He'd panicked and brought Elizabeth straight in to see Doc Harrison, not thinking beyond the baby's immediate needs.

"If it's okay with you," he said, "after I bring in Lizzie's stuff, I'll take a quick run out there and put the dogs in the barn. I can pick up a toothbrush and a razor while I'm at it, and call Len down the road. He could run over and feed all the animals in the morning."

"That's fine." *A toothbrush and a razor.* The announced items made his impending presence in her house more real, and she shivered again.

"Thank you, Gwen. This means more than I can say." He looked around at the house as if seeing it for the first time. "It's real nice here."

"I like it."

"And something smells great."

"Oh! The cinnamon rolls!" She'd totally forgotten them. Talk about being preoccupied. She *never* forgot what was in the oven, which was why she never bothered to set a timer. She hurried forward and put Elizabeth into his arms. "Hold her for a minute."

"Sure."

She got the rolls out in the nick of time. They were plump and golden-brown, oozing with warm raisins and caramelized sugar. She set them on the counter to cool and went to retrieve Elizabeth.

"Are those for something in particular?" Travis asked as he handed over the baby.

"No. I just felt like making them." She cradled Elizabeth against her shoulder and patted her back.

"Gonna put frosting on them?"

"I always do." She couldn't help smiling at the longing in his eyes when he glanced over at the rolls. "I'd be willing to share them, if you like."

He grinned. "I'd like. If a guy's gonna be noble, he oughta at least get a consolation prize."

Before she could think of an answer, he was out the door headed for his truck. And it appeared he hadn't completely forgotten about his sexual needs, after all.

WHEN TRAVIS drove up to Gwen's house a second time, he'd calmed down considerably, enough to notice things. Although he'd driven past this two-story Victorian lots of times, he'd never paid much attention to it because Gwen had seemed like a stuck-up woman with a stuck-up house. Funny how things worked out. As of now, they were both the answer to his prayers.

The house he'd always considered too fussy had become the prettiest place on the block because it was only a short drive from Doc Harrison's office, and because Gwen was allowing him to stay here with Lizzie. Two weeks ago he would have said the exterior paint job made the house look like a goddamned Christmas tree, but this afternoon, he thought the grayish-green siding and the red-orange gingerbread trim were just about perfect.

He even liked the canary-yellow she'd used here and there as an accent color. In a week or two the daffodils would be blooming in the flower garden, which would go real good with the yellow on the posts and along the eaves. A couple of blue spruces that looked as old as the house stood on either side of her walkway, and he took a deep, appreciative breath as he went up to the porch.

The wicker porch furniture might be a little too girlie for him, but it looked comfortable, and when he rang the doorbell, it had a nice, deep chime to it. Best of all, he could still smell those cinnamon rolls.

Gwen answered the door by herself, without Lizzie.

The old panic came back and he moved quickly into the house. "Where is she?"

"I finally got her to sleep. I don't know how long it'll last, but for now—"

"Let me see. I want to make sure she's breathing."

"If you wake her up, so help me, I'll throttle you. It took me forever to get her to drift off."

"I won't wake her up! Where is she?"

"Upstairs."

Still carrying his duffel bag with his overnight stuff in it, he started toward the staircase just beyond the entry hall.

"Wait a minute!" She grabbed his arm. "You sound like a herd of buffalo. Take off your boots."

"Oh, for crying out loud." He set down his duffel, grabbed the newel post and quickly tugged off his boots. Then he took the stairs two at a time. When he got to the top, he realized he had no idea which bedroom she was in. He spun around and nearly knocked Gwen back down the stairs. "Sorry." He steadied her before she could take a header. "Which room?"

"The first one on the left," she murmured. "And keep your voice down."

He glanced at the closed bedroom door and saw little puffs of smoke coming underneath it. "It's on fire!"

"No!" Gwen clutched his arm. "Damn it, you're going to wake her up. That's not smoke, it's steam from the humidifier. I set it up in there so she could breathe easier."

"Oh." He glanced down at her. "Sorry. But you should have warned me."

"You bought the thing. I figured you'd know what it did."

"How would I know? If I get sick, I just drink some Jack Daniel's and I'm right as rain."

She gazed at him. "Then I'm very glad I'm helping you take care of Elizabeth. We're not dosing her with alcohol."

"Of course we're not. I'm not stupid." Without waiting to see if she'd agree or disagree, he headed for the closed door and eased it open. Steam billowed out, and he could hear the hiss of the machine. He wished it didn't remind him of going through a haunted house back when he was a kid. He hadn't been very manly going through that foggy place, and he didn't feel particularly manly now, facing this illness of Lizzie's.

If she really was asleep in this clouded-up room, that was a good thing. But she was a greenhorn when it came to this head cold business, and he kept wondering if she knew how to breathe out of her mouth or if she could somehow get mucus stuck in her throat and choke. He wasn't sure if you were born knowing how to deal with mucus.

Once inside the room, he knew for a fact she was breathing. He could hear her rasping away, poor little baby. He crept over to the fancy white crib in the corner of the bedroom and stopped just short of it to study her.

Sure enough, she was asleep on her tummy, her little bottom pushed up in the air the way she'd taken to doing. She was breathing through her mouth, so at least he could relax on that score. She was drooling onto the sheet and her cheeks looked flushed.

Damn, but he wanted her to be better. He'd give anything if he could be sick instead of her. A cold was no problem for him. He'd like to get his hands on the idiot who had come to the wedding spreading germs to this little, innocent baby. That person should be strung up.

"Satisfied?" Gwen whispered.

He turned and realized Gwen was standing beside him. He also realized something he'd been too worried to notice when he came through the door. She wasn't dressed in the old sweats she'd had on when he'd arrived the first time. Instead she wore a white silky blouse buttoned just to the swell of her cleavage, and green slacks that fit her behind in an outstanding way. And her long, glossy hair was down around her shoulders. And there was red lipstick on those soft, kissable lips.

His body stirred and tightened. Vaguely he remembered promising something in order to get Gwen to let him stay here. As he stared at her, he finally remembered what it was. He'd promised to behave himself.

6

VANITY HAD GOTTEN the better of her, Gwen had to admit. Even in the misty twilight created by the late afternoon and fog from the humidifier, she could see the change in Travis's expression as he looked at her, really looked at her, for the first time.

She should have stayed in her old sweats, which sent the message that she wasn't interested. She would have stayed in her grubbies, too, if Elizabeth hadn't gone to sleep. But once the baby had drifted off, Gwen had glanced in the beveled mirror that hung above the bedroom's antique dresser and winced at her ragtag appearance.

She'd tried to talk herself out of changing clothes the entire time she spent frosting the cinnamon rolls. She'd continued the internal discussion while she washed up the dishes she'd used and took a container of her homemade lasagna out of the freezer for dinner. But when she'd done every imaginable chore in the kitchen and Travis still hadn't arrived, she gave up the fight and went into her private suite off the kitchen to put on a different outfit.

Once she'd started the transformation, she hadn't been able to stop primping. She'd brushed and curled her hair and put on makeup. She'd even taken an emery board to her fingernails. Any bystander would assume she had a hot date coming up.

As the mist swirled around them, Travis shoved back his hat and looked his fill. Under his scrutiny, she was embarrassed to be caught going to so much trouble to look good. "I could use a cup of coffee," she murmured, and started out of the room.

"Yeah, me, too." His voice sounded husky.

As she went down the stairs, she heard the click of the bedroom door as he closed it behind him.

"Which room is mine?" he called softly. "I'll put my duffel in there." Intimate whispers. A shared roof. A common concern. An explosive combination.

"The one next to Elizabeth's," she said over her shoulder.

"Where's yours?"

She paused, her hand on the banister, her heart hammering. She didn't turn around, but she could feel his gaze on her. "Why?"

"Idle curiosity."

She didn't think there was anything idle about it, but his question was her own stupid fault. She hadn't been able to stand the thought of appearing dowdy in his presence, but she'd changed the rules when she'd changed clothes. Now she'd have to deal with his renewed sex drive. She turned to glance up at him and hoped her expression gave nothing away. She needed to regain a measure of control over the situation, and she wouldn't do it by acknowledging that his question meant anything at all. "I have a suite downstairs," she said in a matter-of-fact tone, "so that I have some privacy when I have guests."

He nodded, his expression bland. "Good idea."

"I'll go make that coffee." Quickening her pace, she descended the stairs and headed for the kitchen. Not that she was escaping anything by doing so. She'd barely started the coffee brewing when he appeared, minus his duffel and his hat.

And with a gleam in his eye. "Sure smells great in here, between the cinnamon rolls and the coffee," he said.

"Thanks." As she busied herself getting cups and saucers from the cupboard, she adopted her best hostess manner—friendly but reserved. "I could serve you in the library, if you'd like."

"You don't have to *serve* me at all." He walked over to the counter where the cinnamon rolls were still in their pans. "I can have some of these, right?"

"As many as you want."

"Good." He picked up one of the pans, reached inside and tore a roll free with his fingers, stirring up the sweet yeasty aroma. Then he lifted it in her direction. "Here's to you." Then he took a big bite, closed his eyes and moaned in satisfaction.

Desire slammed into her, and the cups and saucers she held rattled in her grip.

He opened his eyes and gazed at her as he chewed slowly and swallowed. "This is so good, it's probably illegal," he said before taking another bite.

"P-people usually like them." Terrific. She was stuttering. And blushing, if the heat in her cheeks was any clue. She was also in danger of dropping the delicate cups and saucers in her hand. To prevent that, she set them down on the sturdy work table in the middle of the kitchen.

Crossing to the coffeepot, she picked up the carafe. The next logical step would be to actually pour coffee into the cups, but she was quivering too much to do that yet, so she stalled. "How do you like your coffee?"

"With cream, if you have some. Damn, these rolls are good." He finished off his first one and licked the stickiness from his fingers.

The action of his tongue gave her another jolt that settled with swift determination between her thighs. "I have cream." She turned in relief to the refrigerator and opened the door. The cool air felt wonderful against her heated skin. If she stood there a moment, maybe she'd regain her composure.

She was probably acting like an idiot, but surely any red-blooded woman would be in turmoil after watching his reaction after taking a bite of a cinnamon roll. And the sensuous way he'd licked his fingers belonged in an X-rated movie. Travis eating a cinnamon roll was the most erotic thing she'd ever seen.

"If you're out, that's okay."

"Out?" She realized that she'd totally forgotten why she'd opened the refrigerator in the first place.

"Of cream."

Cream. She'd been staring at the container for at least thirty seconds without seeing it. "It's right here. I was taking a little inventory of my supplies while I was at it." She pulled the cream carton from the shelf and closed the refrigerator door with careful efficiency.

"Gwen, are you okay?"

She turned to him with what she hoped was a pleasant smile, an easygoing smile, perhaps even a jaunty smile. "I'm fine."

He gestured behind her. "The reason I ask is that you just put the coffee in the refrigerator."

Hot embarrassment flooded through her. "Oh, dear." She plopped the cream on the counter and jerked open the refrigerator door. Sure enough, the coffee carafe sat on the top shelf where the cream had been.

"Iced coffee is good, too." He was right behind her, and his voice was dangerously close to her ear.

"I want it hot." She grabbed the carafe and realized what she'd said. "My coffee," she amended quickly. "I like hot coffee."

"I like it any way I can get it." His body brushed hers and his spicy scent teased her senses as he reached around her and nudged the refrigerator door closed.

Her pulse raced and the carafe trembled in her grip. "Be careful," she said, her voice quivering. "I have hot coffee here."

"Are you about to throw it on me?" He drew her hair aside and nibbled at her earlobe.

She gulped for air as the gentle rake of his teeth drove her insane. "Travis, this isn't what I—"

"You fixed yourself up for me," he murmured as he caressed the nape of her neck. "Don't tell me this isn't what you want. We both know better."

"I don't know what I was thinking!" she wailed. Her knees threatened to give way as he kissed the tender spot behind her ear.

"Then let me tell you what you were thinking." His warm breath tickled her skin as he slid his arm around her waist and drew her back until she made easy but definite contact with his erection. "You were thinking that we wouldn't be taking care of Lizzie every minute." He cupped her breast softly, teasingly. "You were thinking that we might need a way to pass the time." Only a slight tremble in his voice betrayed his excitement. Otherwise he seemed in perfect control.

She groaned and closed her eyes. The quiver in his

voice told her he was going wild inside, as she was. Yet he touched her with such finesse, such exquisite restraint. He must know that when a woman was completely aroused, a light caress had more power than a heavy hand. Oh, yes. He knew that a slow approach would hypnotize, robbing her of the will to resist. Of course he knew. He was an expert at this sort of thing.

Her mind emptied of everything except his hand at her breast, his lips brushing the outer rim of her ear. Her body grew as limp and cooperative as a rag doll's. "I'm...going to drop this...coffeepot," she whispered.

"No, you're not." His voice was tight with strain as he took the carafe from her nerveless fingers. It clicked down on the kitchen table behind him.

"Travis—"

His breathing harshened. "You're going to let me love you." He slipped a silk-covered button of her blouse from its loop.

"No," she said softly, knowing it was a token protest that meant nothing. He was in command.

"Yes," he murmured.

Her heart raced with anticipation. The house was completely, utterly still, except for the fevered rasp of their breathing. Travis took his time, dropping butterfly kisses along her shoulder as her blouse gradually fell away. Another button gave way, and another. Her breasts ached with the need to be touched.

And then a baby's cough broke the silence.

Travis's hand stilled.

Elizabeth coughed again and started to cry.

Travis kissed Gwen's neck firmly and quickly, then released her. Without a word he left the kitchen and started up the stairs.

Fumbling to refasten her blouse, Gwen followed him on wobbly legs as the baby's coughs became louder and her wails higher pitched. She met Travis coming down the stairs with a flushed and unhappy Elizabeth in his arms.

"What can we do?" he asked.

"Try cleaning out her nose and giving her some juice, I guess."

"She feels hot."

"We'll take her temperature, then. I have a thermometer in my bathroom. Bring her in there." She retraced her steps back through the kitchen and opened the door into her suite.

When the house was built at the turn of the century, the rooms had been used as maid's quarters. Gwen had a small sitting room, a bedroom and a bathroom that were off-limits to guests. She'd meant to keep them off-limits to Travis, too, yet the scene in the kitchen had demonstrated how easily she could give up her promises to herself.

"Try rocking her in the rocker while I get the thermometer." She hurried into her bathroom and took the thermometer out of an oak cabinet. A couple of years ago she'd replaced her old one with a digital model that registered by placing it the patient's ear. She'd justified it as a service for guests with children, but lately she'd begun to realize her "guest" purchases were really for the family she longed for.

The wooden rocking horse in a bedroom upstairs, the toy train on the library mantel and the children's books scattered on shelves throughout the house had all been collected in hopes she'd someday become a mother. If she allowed herself to get sidetracked with a confirmed bachelor like Travis, she was in danger of being involved with him when Mr. Right came along. She really needed to stay away from Travis Evans.

Yet when she walked into the sitting room and found him rocking Elizabeth in the delicate antique chair padded with ruffled chintz cushions, her heart squeezed in a way that didn't bode well for staying away. He cuddled the fussy baby against his broad chest and dabbed at her nose with a tissue he'd taken from a box on the table beside him.

And he was singing to her. Off-key.

He glanced up and grinned sheepishly. "I'm a lousy singer, but Lizzie never seems to care. It usually helps her quiet down."

Gwen swallowed the lump in her throat. It wasn't fair that a man who was so good with women and children should refuse to become a husband. "I'm sure it does." She walked over to the rocker and crouched beside it. "Let's see what her temperature is." Murmuring to the baby, she eased the thermometer cautiously into her outer ear.

"Doc Harrison has one like that, too."

His voice rippled over her nerve endings. He could probably recite names from the phone book and get a response from her. Or from any woman. Perhaps that bothered her the most—knowing he'd used his seductive techniques on so many other lovers. She longed to believe that the chemistry between her and Travis was unique, but that would be fooling herself, which was a dangerous thing to do.

She glanced at the numbers on the thermometer. "A hundred degrees. That's not too bad."

"You're sure that thing's working?"

"Pretty sure."

"Test it on me to make sure. It could be broken." He

cupped his hand around Elizabeth's soft cheek. "She feels hot to me."

"Okay. Let me sterilize it first." She returned to the bathroom and tried not to think of the tender way his fingers had curved around Elizabeth's cheek. Gwen ached with longing. Travis's touch against her bare skin would be heaven...and hell, because he would be a temporary lover.

After she'd sterilized the tip of the thermometer, she returned to the sitting room and crouched beside the rocker again. "Hold still. This might tickle."

He angled his head. "I'm not ticklish. Do it." He continued to stroke the baby's cheek, and it seemed to have a calming effect on her. She still coughed every so often, but she stopped crying.

It wasn't surprising, Gwen thought as she prepared to insert the thermometer in his ear. Travis had an amazing ability to get females to do what he wanted them to do. He was one of the most appealing male specimens she'd ever known.

Even his ears were attractive. She liked the way his thick brown hair fell into a soft wave right there. As she slid the thermometer carefully into the outer channel, she imagined finger-combing his hair back and outlining the curve of his ear with her tongue. It wasn't an appropriate thought considering he was holding a sick baby, but Travis inspired inappropriate thoughts.

And he definitely had nicely formed ears. She suspected that everything about Travis was nicely formed. Her womb tightened at the thought.

"Mmm." He closed his eyes. "Feels sort of sexy."

"That's because you think everything feels sexy."

"Just about everything does, if you do it right."

Zing. A painfully sweet sensation settled between her thighs. "Ninety-eight-point-six," she said as calmly as she could manage. She lifted the thermometer from his ear. "It's working." She stood and moved away from his commanding force field.

He gazed down at Elizabeth and sighed. "I wish I could do some hocus-pocus and get her well."

"It's a cliché, but love is sometimes the best medicine."

Travis looked up at her. "Then she'll be better real quick. I'm crazy about this little kid."

Gwen experienced a sudden and unworthy stab of jealousy. She was ashamed of herself, resenting his feelings for Elizabeth. Gwen loved the baby, too, and was thrilled that Travis was so devoted to her. After all, Elizabeth had a tough situation—a mother on the run and an uncertain family future, depending on who her father was. The baby needed all the luck and love she could get.

Gwen laid down the thermometer. "Why don't I go upstairs and get the suction bulb so we can take care of her nose? Then we'll give her some juice."

"Is it okay if I stay here? She's used to the rocker at the ranch, and I think this makes her feel more at home."

"Sure. I'll be right back." As Gwen left the room, she wondered if she'd ever find a man with Travis's obvious capacity to love...and a desire to stay.

LIZZIE WASN'T the only one who felt at home in this cozy suite of rooms, Travis thought. Gwen had a real gift for putting things together so a person felt welcome. He pictured sharing a meal at the drop-leaf table, or enjoying some serious cuddling on the love seat in front of the small fireplace.

Sure, the decoration scheme was a little flowery, but even though he was a guy, flowers appealed to him. Actually they had the potential to get him hot. Flowers had always seemed like sex symbols to him.

Besides, he liked the idea of making love to a woman in her surroundings. It felt as if he'd penetrated her inner sanctum, breached the last of her defenses, touched the core of who she was. That turned him on.

He'd always been careful, though, not to let a woman touch the core of who *he* was. Maybe that wasn't fair, but it was the way things had to be. He could afford to fall in lust, but not in love.

From that standpoint, Gwen made him nervous. His need for her felt different, more urgent, less manageable than his other affairs. At the beginning of a relationship, he usually pictured the end of it and started preparing for that inevitable day. But the end of this relationship wouldn't come into focus for him.

In his lap, Lizzie coughed. He lifted her to his shoulder and patted her back as she coughed again. Poor little tyke. He didn't approve of a system that let babies catch colds. If he was in charge of the world, nobody would get sick until they were at least twenty-one and could treat it with booze.

Maybe Lizzie was throwing off his normal sense of timing with Gwen, he thought. It sure was possible, especially considering how Lizzie's illness made him feel raw inside. Maybe he only thought he needed Gwen more because she represented help with the baby.

Then again, maybe it was those damned cinnamon

rolls. He'd never tasted anything so fantastic in his life. They were almost as good as sex. Almost.

Gwen came back into the room holding a small towel and a basin with the suction doohickey inside it. There was nothing deliberately sexy about the way she moved, and there was definitely nothing sexy about the job she proposed to do. He winced thinking about it, in fact. And yet he couldn't stop looking at the swell of her breasts or the curve of her hips. She was so womanly he could barely stand it.

She picked up one of the two ladder-backed chairs flanking the drop-leaf table and carried it over next to the rocker. "She probably isn't going to like this."

Travis eyed the rubber bulb with suspicion. "Then let's skip it. What if you suck out something important?"

She smiled. "I don't think that's possible. I read the directions, and we're not applying much pressure. And if we don't do this, she'll have trouble drinking from a bottle."

"I know. This morning I tried to teach her to blow out of her nose, but she didn't get the picture. She can sneeze, but she can't blow yet. I showed her about twenty times, but she just stared at me."

"She's just too little for some of these tricks. Come on, let's try this thing. Prop her up in your lap."

"Okay." Travis surrendered to the inevitable. The doc had said they needed to get some fluids in the baby, and she couldn't drink as long as her nose was plugged. "Here we go, Lizzie." He propped her so she was facing Gwen. "Remember, this isn't me doing this. It's your mean Auntie Gwen."

"Thank you, Benedict Arnold." Gwen picked up the bulb.

Travis cringed. "This is a gross concept, you know that?"

"Then don't watch."

"I don't believe I will." By turning his head to the right, he could look at Gwen's cleavage, instead. That was an excellent distraction until Lizzie started to yell. He glanced back at the sputtering, red-faced baby as Gwen pulled away from her. "Hey! You hurt her."

"She probably didn't like the sensation, but one nostril is free. Hold her so I can do the other one."

"But listen to her! She hates this."

"She'll be happier when she can breathe again." Gwen looked him in the eye. "She won't go through her life pain and hassle-free, Travis. Sometimes she'll have to suffer a little in order to make progress."

"Says who?"

Gwen smiled and shook her head. "It's a fact of life."

"Not when I'm around."

"Then it's a good thing you won't ever see a woman give birth. You'd probably outlaw the process forever."

Travis had thought about what women had to go through to bring kids into the world, about what Jessica had gone through, alone, to produce Lizzie. The concept did make him flinch and feel slightly sick to his stomach.

"You might be right," he said. Then he gazed at Lizzie. "But I would have given anything to see her born," he added quietly.

7

ONE BY ONE, Travis was knocking down Gwen's preconceived ideas about him. The man she'd thought she knew would never have admitted regret at not being there when his baby was born. She'd been attracted to him when she thought he was sexy but not very sensitive. Sexy *and* sensitive might be more than she could handle.

She finished cleaning out Elizabeth's nose. "There. Now let's try a bottle of juice."

"Would you be able to take her for a little while?" Travis asked. "My arm is cramping up. Old steer wrestling injury."

"Sure thing." She set down the basin and lifted Elizabeth into her arms. The baby's breathing was still wheezy, but sounded a little clearer than it had before.

"That's better." Travis stood, rolled his shoulder and flexed his fingers. "It stiffens up on me if I stay in one position too long." He held out his arms. "I can take her back now, if you want."

"That's okay. I'll feed her." Once again, Gwen had been caught staring, fascinated by the ripple of muscles when he rolled his shoulder and the grace in those long, talented fingers. And if she wasn't mistaken, he'd just admitted a physical weakness, a very unmacho thing to do. "Have you ever tried massage?" she asked.

He glanced at her, that gleam back in his eyes. "Are you offering?"

She swallowed. "Uh, no." She sat down in the rocker, positioned the towel over her shoulder and propped Elizabeth there, so the baby could breathe easier. The seat cushion still held Travis's warmth, and Gwen began to tingle in a very specific spot. "I don't really know anything about massage."

"I do. I could teach you what to do."

She just bet he could. She wished she'd waited to sit down until the rocker cushion had cooled off. The heat he'd left there was doing things to her that made her blush. "We'll see. Better go get her bottle of juice ready before she plugs up again. I put all that stuff in the kitchen."

"I saw it. Be right back."

Once he was out the door she sighed and relaxed back against the rocker. She would get through this episode one moment at a time and hope, for her own sake, that she didn't end up in bed with this man.

She adjusted Elizabeth's position against her shoulder to give the little girl maximum chance to breathe without so much effort. Elizabeth coughed and laid her head on Gwen's shoulder.

"You're exhausted, aren't you, sweetheart?" Gwen murmured. "Can't sleep, can't eat. It's almost like being in love." She had the unwelcome thought that she hadn't been sleeping or eating well recently, either.

"Who's in love?" Travis asked as he came back with the bottle of apple juice in his hand.

"Matty and Sebastian," Gwen answered quickly. She settled Elizabeth in the crook of her arm and took the bottle Travis handed her. "I've never seen two people so much in love." She offered the bottle to Elizabeth, and the baby took the nipple, which was a good sign.

Travis snorted. "They're not only in love, they're in la-la land. It got so I had to keep a close eye on ol' Sebastian, because his mind wasn't on his work. Twice he dumped oats in the watering trough, which made a hellacious mess."

"I know what you mean." Gwen kept her attention on Elizabeth, and although the baby snuffled a little while she drank, she was drinking, which was the main thing. "When Matty and I went to Canon City to look for clothes, she was driving down the street raving about how wonderful Sebastian is and nearly stripped the gears on her truck."

Travis blew out a breath. "I was wondering why her truck wasn't shifting so smooth. I ran it yesterday so it wouldn't sit idle all week. I'll bet she's got some teeth missing in those gears."

"It's possible." Gwen smiled, remembering how excited and totally brainless Matty had been in those last few days before the wedding.

"I have to say this love business is scary," Travis said.

Gwen glanced up. "I take it you've never…"

"Not to the point where I'd start rubbing Bag Balm on the hood of my truck, thinking it was car wax. Sebastian did that, too." He paused. "I guess you've been in love, seeing as how you got married."

Gwen thought about Derek. She'd been crazy about him once. Love had made her blind, deaf and dumb. "I have been in love." She gazed down at Elizabeth. "If you're lucky, you fall for someone who feels the same about you."

"Hey, he must have if he asked you to marry him."

"Maybe he did, in his own way, but he wasn't the faithful type." Gwen tilted the bottle a fraction to keep the apple juice flowing. "Unfortunately he didn't realize that until after he put a ring on my finger."

"Do you still love him?"

The roughened timbre of his voice made her look up. If she didn't know better, she'd swear he was worried about her answer. Yet he shouldn't care if she still loved Derek or not. Sex and love were two different things to Travis, and he only wanted one of them from her.

Before she could answer, Elizabeth began to cough and gag.

Gwen immediately handed the bottle to Travis and hoisted the baby to her shoulder again. She patted her firmly as the baby continued to cough and wheeze.

"Is she okay?" Travis hovered near. "Want me to call the doc?"

"I think she got some down the wrong drain." She stood and walked back and forth with Elizabeth, jiggling and patting.

Eventually the baby's coughing became a burp. Then she began taking shallow, raspy breaths.

"Do you think her fever's worse?" Travis came close and laid his hand over Elizabeth's forehead. "Maybe we should take her temperature again."

"Let's wait a bit on that," Gwen said. Having Travis so close made her tremble, even when he was only there to check on the baby. She put some distance between them. "I really think she just needs time to fight this. Maybe we should try changing her and putting her down again."

"I'll do that. Let me take her." He scooped her out of Gwen's arms.

In the process he brushed a hand across her breast. Gwen was sure it was an accident. The touch was too casual to be intentional. When Travis wanted to caress a woman, he wouldn't be sly about it. Still, the contact made her nipple pucker in reaction.

"I'll come upstairs with you," she said, following him through the kitchen and into the hallway. As long as she concentrated on the sick child, she could resist him, she told herself. "I want to try putting a rolled blanket under the crib mattress, to elevate the bed so she won't be so horizontal. I think she might be able to breathe easier that way."

"Good idea." His sock feet whispered over the carpet runner on the stairs and a loose board squeaked under his weight. "You should fix that."

"Actually I sort of like it. A squeaky step lets me know when my guests are coming downstairs. That way they don't catch me by surprise." And that would go for Travis, too, she thought. A squeak from the stairs tonight and she'd know she was in trouble.

"Have you ever had anybody stay here that worried you?"

"No." *Not until now.* "I check on the people who make reservations. If I find anything suspicious, I call them back and tell them I've made a mistake and I'm full at that time."

"That's good, but it might not be enough. If word gets out that you're running the place alone...."

"I know some basic self-defense techniques." Gwen didn't know how to take his obvious concern for her safety. On a surface level, she wanted to brush it off as being condescending and typically male. But on a deeper level she liked it. Derek had always assumed she could take care of herself, and she could, but there was something gratifying about a man who took a protective stance.

"I think a dog would be a great idea." He turned left into Elizabeth's bedroom. "A big dog."

"I don't have much of a yard." Gwen followed him and went over to retrieve the blanket that lay folded across the foot of the room's queen-size bed.

"No problem. Take Fido for runs in the park. Or bring him out when you come to see Matty and Sebastian." Travis put Elizabeth on her back in the crib and she began to complain. "Hey, Lizzie, what's up, kid?" He levered the side down and started unsnapping the baby's sleeper. "Easy does it, darlin'. Got to change your britches."

Travis was so casual about the future, Gwen thought. When she came out to visit Matty and Sebastian, he'd said. And when she did, Travis would be there every summer, because in addition to being one of Sebastian's best friends, he now worked for the combined spreads. Travis would be in her future as long as she remained friends with Matty and Sebastian. If Travis became her lover, no matter how long it lasted, he would be a very complicated part of that future.

She held the blanket to her chest as she watched him change Elizabeth's diaper with efficient movements. He'd obviously taken the time to learn how so he'd be as proficient at this as he was at everything else he chose to do.

With no difficulty he found what he needed in the diaper bag, and he kept the baby so constantly entertained she had little time to fuss. When her sleeper was off, he leaned down and vibrated his lips against her tummy. Sick as she was, she began to chuckle and make little crowing noises.

Travis always seemed to know the right sensual move to make, Gwen thought. A touch, a kiss, or a teasing caress always came at the right moment. His timing was impeccable.

He fished a bedraggled sock monkey out of the diaper bag and gave it to Elizabeth to hold. "Look who I found! Bruce!"

The baby squealed in delight and waved the monkey around, whapping it against Travis's cheek.

"You missed your Bruce, didn't you?" Travis said. "No wonder you couldn't sleep."

"Shoot, I didn't even think about looking in the bag for that monkey," Gwen said. "He's bound to help the situation."

"Gotta have Bruce," Travis said as he took off the wet diaper.

"I found out Sebastian used to have a sock monkey named Bruce," Gwen said. "Now that he's named this one Bruce, I suppose when Elizabeth has kids, she'll give them a sock monkey named Bruce. A hundred years from now, her descendants will still be getting sock monkeys named Bruce."

Travis's movements stilled and he glanced over his shoulder at Gwen. "Good Lord. If Lizzie is really my kid, then some day I could be a granddaddy."

Gwen couldn't help chuckling at the astonishment in his expression. "Does that prospect horrify you?"

"No," he said thoughtfully. He turned back to his work. "No, it doesn't horrify me. It probably should, but it doesn't."

Gwen longed to have him explain exactly why he'd decided not to get married. From her viewpoint, he was ripe for such a commitment. But he'd be suspicious of a question like that coming from her, so she didn't ask it.

"Here's a blanket to tuck under the head of the crib mattress," she said, laying it on the top of the dresser next to the crib. "I'm going to get more water for the humidifier and then I'll see about some dinner for us."

"That would be great." He glanced over at her. "I'm feeling a lot calmer about Lizzie than I was a few hours ago. Thanks for all you've done."

"I haven't done much."

"You were here when I needed you."

The words were more potent than he probably meant them to be, she thought. "Glad I could be of help." Then she left the room before she said or did something really dumb.

AN HOUR LATER Travis had polished off a second helping of lasagna and wondered if he had room for a cinnamon roll or two for dessert. Gwen could cook like nobody's business, and he'd gotten a kick out of eating off of antique china in her small formal dining room.

He'd checked on Lizzie in between courses of lasagna, and she was sleeping pretty soundly. Gwen had put on a new pot of coffee and the atmosphere in the house was downright cozy.

He glanced across the table at Gwen. During the meal he'd managed to find out a little about her folks and gathered that they'd pressured her to do something more high-toned than run a bed and breakfast in a small town like Huerfano. He thought Gwen and this place were a perfect fit, and she seemed to love the role of hostess. He hoped she wouldn't let her folks talk her into selling the house and becoming scholarly like them, or a big-city hotshot like her brother. She seemed cut out for this life.

Besides, Huerfano would be a sadder place if Gwen ever left it, he thought. He didn't like the idea at all.

He laid his cloth napkin beside his plate. "You're something, you know that?"

"I'm really not going to bed with you," she said quietly. "So you can just stop giving me that look."

He laughed in surprise. "What look?"

"Don't you suppose I can see what's going on in that fertile mind of yours? You were smiling that smile. Tell me you weren't sitting over there thinking of how to maneuver us into bed, now that Elizabeth's asleep and dinner's over."

Never mind that for most of the meal he'd been contemplating exactly what she'd just accused him of. At this very minute he'd been thinking very pure thoughts, and he reacted with the outrage of the innocent. "I was thinking how well you run this bed and breakfast!"

"Oh, right. I believe the word *bed* figured into your scheme, but the rest of it is horse manure."

He'd never been a fan of defensive tactics. In any tussle, he preferred going on the offense as quickly as possible. He leaned forward. "Since you've brought up the subject, let's talk about your outfit."

Wariness lit her dark eyes. "It's nothing special."

"Oh, really? When I first arrived this afternoon you were in a baggy old sweat suit."

"You caught me by surprise."

"I realize that." And her clothes wouldn't have made any difference to him. He would have been turned on by seeing her in sweats, once the immediate danger had passed with Lizzie, but he decided not to say that and prejudice his case. "Anyway, I come back later to find you in a silky blouse and snug-fitting pants. Your hair is down and you have on lipstick. What's that supposed to mean?"

Her cheeks grew very pink. "Probably a knee-jerk reaction to having guests. I'm in the habit of getting fixed up when someone's going to be here overnight."

"I'm not a guest," he said softly. "Or would you like me to pay for tonight? If so, name your price. I'd be happy to empty my bank account for what you've done for Lizzie."

"Of course I don't want you to pay! Don't be ridiculous. I'm doing this to help out with Elizabeth while Matty and Sebastian are gone. You know that."

"I thought I did. You've turned me down flat twice now, so I figured in return for your cooperation with Lizzie, you'd expect me to keep my hands off you. And that's what I promised. Then I saw how you were dressed when I came back from the ranch, and I took another look at the whole program."

She was blushing furiously by this point. "All right! So I didn't want to spend the evening with you looking like a scrub woman. Is that such a crime? I have some pride in my personal appearance, and I—"

"Stop playing games. It doesn't suit you. You want me to want you, Gwen."

She stared at him and her throat moved in a nervous swallow.

That nervous movement caused a wave of tenderness to sweep over him. "It's okay," he murmured. "I'm flattered that you do. And no question about it, I want you. But fair is fair. You can't wave a red cape in front of a bull and not expect him to charge."

She threw down her napkin and pushed back her chair. "And you love to get women to wave that red cape, don't you? You present a challenge they can't resist, and it's not fair to do that, either, considering your agenda!"

"I don't know what you mean. I'm always up-front about—"

"Oh, yes, you certainly are!" She stood, and her voice quivered. "And you think that makes it all right, don't you? You issue your famous disclaimer. You make sure that a woman knows she might satisfy you for a while, but eventually you'll leave her, because *nobody* is woman enough for you."

"That's not true. I—"

"It's absolutely true." Her dark eyes flashed. "To even be considered for the short-term with you is supposed to be an honor, isn't it? And I fell for that kind of thinking, which is why I changed clothes! God help me, I wanted to join the Travis Evans fan club!"

He couldn't believe she so completely misunderstood him. "You've got it backward. The women in my life have been too good for *me*."

She rolled her eyes. "Oh, I'm sure."

"I swear, I leave for their benefit, not mine! Some guys are thoroughbreds, good for the long race, a lifetime together. When it comes to relationships, I'm a quarterhorse!"

"Try telling that to Donna. Do you think she's convinced that she's too good for you, and that's why you dropped her?"

He stood and braced both hands on the table. "I did *not drop her.* I never drop a lady. Never. When I think she's getting too serious, I ease back a little. If she still comes on strong and starts dragging me past the jewelry store window, I have a talk with her."

"How considerate."

"I think it is!" His blood was pumping now. Too bad he was also getting aroused. That was inconvenient. "I try to keep things like they were. If she can't do that, I send her a dozen roses and let her know that we can't go on like we have been, but she'll always be in my heart."

"Your heart must look like a Denver freeway at rush hour!"

He shoved away from the table, more wound than he wanted her to know. She made him out to be some arrogant bastard, when all he'd ever wanted was to bring women pleasure. "I cherish every woman I've ever made love to."

"A friend of mine cherishes her Beanie Babies, too." Gwen crossed her arms. "At last count, she had two hundred and sixteen of those suckers."

"I have not made love to two hundred and sixteen women, damn it!"

"Yet! Give you time. You're a collector, as much as my friend is, and I'll be damned if I'm going to be part of that collection."

"Fine with me." But it wasn't. The fire in her made him want to grab her and kiss her senseless. Normally, when a woman got this uppity, especially before they'd even made love, he gave it up as not worth the hassle. He couldn't seem to walk away from Gwen, though. He wanted to convince her that he was a good guy. And that was a bad sign.

She tossed her head, and her glossy dark hair shone in the light from the crystal chandelier. "I'll admit that you tempt me, both because you're sexy as hell and because you present a challenge."

Maybe that's all she was to him, too, he thought. A challenge. Until now he'd batted a thousand. Whenever he'd put as much effort into a woman as he had with Gwen, he'd ended up in bed with her. There had been no exceptions. But he'd been good to those ladies, damn it. He'd treated them right, and he'd let them down easy. Lots of guys, including her ex, hadn't been so careful.

She wasn't finished ripping him a new one, though. "Around these parts," she said, "if you're an eligible female it's bad enough to be loved and left by the great Travis Evans, but at least you know you made the grade. It's a real blow to be passed over completely. So, at least I have it on record that you want me."

And he did. Still. Even after she'd drawn and quartered him.

She fixed him with a bold stare. "I think I'll just quit while I'm ahead."

Rejected. Again. Hell. He worked hard to look nonchalant about it. "Does that mean you do or do not want help with the dishes?"

8

IF THE DOORBELL hadn't chimed at that moment, Gwen was afraid she would have started throwing dishes at Travis instead of asking him to help wash them. And her dishes were carefully gathered antiques, mismatched on purpose and irreplaceable. Her urge to throw them showed just how out of control she'd become when it came to this man.

"Excuse me." As she left the dining room and walked down the hallway to the front door she took a deep breath. Too bad she hadn't been able to just say *no* instead of delivering a dissertation on the subject of Travis's life-style. A simple rejection would have left her with more dignity.

She reached for the doorknob.

"Wait!" Travis called from the dining room door. "Don't open it."

She turned. "Why not?"

He strode down the hall toward her. "Sebastian and I figure whoever's after Jessica might somehow find out about Lizzie and come after her, too."

"Oh." What a ghastly thought. No wonder his mind had been on security measures for her bed and breakfast. "I didn't realize."

"We haven't made a point of saying so, but we're careful. Security is second nature to me at the ranch, but the change of scene made me forget for a minute.

Don't you have one of those peephole things so you can check who's outside?"

"No. It would ruin the look of the door. Besides, in the daytime I can pretty well guess who's out there by looking through the glass. It's only at night that I can't see as well."

Travis blew out a breath. "Then wait a sec." He walked into the parlor on the left, where he moved the curtain aside to check the porch. "It's Donna. Go ahead and let her in."

Donna. Donna sure as hell wasn't paying her a visit, Gwen thought. They were only passing acquaintances. No doubt Travis's truck parked outside had caught the woman's attention. Gwen wondered if the kindergarten teacher had received a dozen kiss-off roses, and if Donna was still in Travis's heart. Chances were good that Donna had once been in Travis's bed, and the thought made Gwen clench her teeth.

She opened the door. "Donna! What a surprise." She stepped back from the doorway. "Come in."

"Excuse me for bothering you, Gwen."

As Donna stepped into the entry, Gwen thought how petite and doll-like she looked. But she also had generous breasts, so the doll she most resembled was Barbie. Maybe gym-teacher Barbie, considering Donna's short, practical haircut.

"No bother." Gwen closed the door.

"I noticed Travis's truck out front and wondered if he happened to be here. I need to talk with him about something and this would save me a trip out to the ranch."

And the woman had apparently forgotten how to dial a phone, Gwen thought.

Travis walked out of the parlor. "What can I do for you, Donna?"

Gwen glanced at him. *Bad choice of words, cowboy.*

"Oh, well, hello, Travis." Donna's cheeks turned pink. Then her gaze dropped to his sock-covered feet and her cheeks were even pinker when she looked up. She shot a furtive glance at Gwen. "I, uh, hope I wasn't interrupting anything."

"Not a thing," Travis said. "I took off my boots so I wouldn't clomp around and wake up Lizzie. She's asleep upstairs."

"Let me take your coat, Donna," Gwen said. When Donna handed it to her, she hooked it on the brass coat tree in the entry. "I have some fresh-baked cinnamon rolls, if you'd like one. And I think there's some coffee left from dinner."

Donna glanced from Gwen to Travis. "You and the baby are staying here?"

"At least for tonight. Lizzie's sick."

"Oh, *no.*"

"'Fraid so. I wanted to be close to Doc Harrison in case we needed him. Gwen was nice enough to let us use a couple of her guest rooms and feed me some dinner."

He seemed awfully eager to clarify that he wasn't sharing a bedroom with his hostess, Gwen thought with some irritation. And he had said he had a rule about being faithful to someone until he moved on. Maybe now that she'd made her position clear, he'd decided to reconnect with Donna.

Well, that was fine with her. Donna could make a fool of herself if she wanted to, but Gwen wasn't planning on it. "Why don't you two go on in the parlor and I'll bring in coffee and cinnamon rolls?" she said.

"That would be very nice." Donna smiled and walked into the parlor. No offer of help, no suggestion that they could all gather in the kitchen. Donna seemed happy to put Gwen in the role of obliging servant and get her out of the way.

"I'll help you," Travis said.

"I wouldn't dream of it." Gwen gave him a scorching look. "Go entertain your guest, Travis."

He lifted his eyebrows, then shrugged and turned to follow Donna into the parlor.

Normally Gwen loved serving people. She drew great satisfaction from arranging a tray with her silver coffeepot, her china sugar and creamer and her antique cups and saucers. Ordinarily serving in the parlor called for lace-trimmed napkins and dainty silver napkin rings. This time she came close to slapping some discount paper napkins on the tray along with the carton of creamer and some old sugar packets from the last time she'd bought take-out coffee at the Huerfano Shop 'n Go.

But she had her pride.

She arranged the tray with more care than usual, in fact. She took time to warm the cinnamon rolls and place them in a linen-draped basket that had an oven-hot stone at the bottom to keep the rolls warm. Fresh coffee, not the leftovers from dinner, went into the silver pot, and she rubbed a spot of tarnish from the handle before she picked up the loaded tray and walked down the hall to the parlor.

She suspected Donna had relished every minute alone with Travis, but if the two of them had had the bad manners to make out on Gwen's fainting couch, she'd order them both out of the house. A person could only be expected to put up with so much.

Bracing herself for a cozy scene, she walked into the parlor and found Travis sitting on the Victorian velvet sofa alone. "Is Donna in the bathroom?" Gwen asked as she set the tray on the table in front of the sofa.

"No, she went home."

Gwen's head came up. "Home? Already?"

"She didn't get the answer she wanted, so she left." He leaned forward. "That smells great. You must have warmed up the rolls."

"Yeah, I did," Gwen said, still perplexed as she glanced at the front door, half-expecting Donna to reappear. "She really went home?"

"She really did. Can I pour this coffee?"

"Sure." Gwen looked at him. "I thought I'd come in here and find the two of you acting very friendly."

He poured the coffee without spilling a drop. "Goes to show what you know. Should I pour you some?"

"Okay." She was dying to know what he'd said that had caused Donna to leave.

He glanced at her. "Are you going to come and sit down or drink it standing up?"

"I'll sit down." She walked around the low table and sat next to him on the crushed velvet as she tried to solve the mystery of Donna's quick exit without having to ask. She had a suspicion the answer had to do with her, which made her heart beat a little faster. It was almost as if Travis wanted to continue to be alone with her.

He poured a dollop of cream into her coffee, gave it a quick stir and put the spoon into his own cup before handing over hers.

"How did you know how I like it?" Her hands weren't entirely steady as she took the coffee.

"I've watched you." He added cream to his cup.

"When?"

"Lots of times." He stirred his coffee with delibera-
tion. "At the wedding reception. Tonight at dinner.
You always take it like that." He tapped his spoon on
the rim of the cup and laid it in the saucer before smiling at her. "Right?"

"Right." She shouldn't be impressed with the fact
that he'd taken the time to notice a small detail like
how she liked her coffee. But she was. "It isn't fair that
you're so darned charming."

He lifted the linen covering on the basket of rolls.
"Donna didn't think I was so darned charming when
I told her I couldn't spend next weekend with her at
her parents' cabin. Oh, God, these smell incredible."

Gwen's insides wouldn't settle down. So Donna
had been here to stake a claim. "I'm sure you could get
away. Matty and Sebastian will be back, and—"

"Oh, I can get away." He paused in the act of taking
a cinnamon roll from the basket and looked up at her.
"But I'm not going to. In spite of all the rotten things
you think about me, I don't use people. Right now
there's only one woman I'm interested in spending the
weekend with."

At the look in his eyes, the jumpiness in her stomach
grew worse. "Travis, I—"

"And just because you won't give me the time of
day doesn't mean I'll grab a good person like Donna
and use her as a substitute. Even when she says she
doesn't mind." He cupped the roll in his hand and
leaned over the basket to take a bite. "Mmm," he murmured. "Mm-mmm."

Gwen gasped. "You *told* her you were interested in
me?"

He swallowed. "Only when she wouldn't back off."

He winked at her. "You might want to avoid her for a while. I don't think you're her favorite person at the moment."

Gwen set her cup and saucer down so she wouldn't drop it. Then she stood and began to pace. "Well, that's it. Now people will assume we're lovers."

"No, they won't. I told Donna you don't think much of me."

"And she told you I was crazy, right?"

"Pretty much." He polished off the cinnamon roll and licked his fingers. "Damn, but those are good. Do you think you could bring some out to the Rocking D once in a while this summer?"

She thought of the tortuous pleasure she would get from doing exactly that—staying for coffee and watching him eat those rolls with his usual gusto. The sensual side of Travis called to her so strongly that she wondered how she'd ever keep him at bay, although she had to. She really had to.

But she couldn't stop seeing Matty and Sebastian because Travis would be there at the ranch. And a gift of cinnamon rolls would be a nice thing to do for the newlyweds.

She threw up her hands. "I might as well. Everyone will expect me to spend a lot of time out there now, chasing after you. I'll be labeled as your summer romance."

"I don't see how you figure that." He picked up his cup and took a swallow of coffee. "Unless you've decided to be my summer romance when I wasn't paying attention."

"You still don't get it, do you? You told Donna you were interested in me. You are staying overnight in my house. No woman in this town will believe that I can resist Travis Evans under those circumstances. Everyone will assume that before the sun comes up, you will have won me over, whether it's true or not."

He gazed at her, a smile lurking in his eyes. "Are you saying I've ruined your reputation?"

"Are you kidding? Women would kill to be in my predicament. I'll bet some would rank spending the night with you above winning the lottery. You haven't ruined my reputation, you've made it. I'll be the envy of every single woman in Fremont County."

"Yeah?" He looked exceedingly pleased with himself. "I'll be damned."

"But before you get too puffed up, let me warn you despite all that, maybe even because of it, I'm not going to bed with you. People can think whatever they want, but when everyone "expects" me to do something, I tend to do the opposite. And you can check with my parents on that one."

He set his cup back in his saucer with a soft little click. "Okay. You've made yourself very plain." He fixed her with a long, penetrating look. "But let's make sure I've got the message. I turn you on, but you don't like the conditions I put on making love, so you'll take a pass. Does that about sum it up?"

She wrapped her arms around her body to keep it still. When he looked at her like that, she had no more willpower than a mushroom. "That pretty much says it all."

He leaned forward, rested his elbows on his knees and wove his fingers together. "Then I get it."

His fingers were so supple and sexy that she couldn't help looking at them with longing. She wouldn't ever know what those fingers could do to her body. But that was for the best.

He gazed at her steadily. "When you told me no at the wedding, I didn't believe you. When you told me no on the phone, I still didn't believe you. But you win, Gwen. I finally believe you. I won't try anything, tonight or anytime. You're safe from me. So you can relax on that score."

Relax? Her stomach was in knots as she struggled with regret. "Good," she said.

"Oh, it could have been." He sounded as sad as she felt. "It really could have been, Gwen."

Didn't she know it. Fairness prompted her to say one more thing. "Maybe you'd...want to call Donna tonight. About next weekend."

He smiled gently and shook his head. "I already explained that thing about substitutes."

"But—"

"I guess you still think I can switch myself from one woman to the next with no problem at all, but—surprise—I can't. Just because I don't plan to try and seduce you anymore doesn't mean I won't want to. It only means I'll control myself. I don't know how long I'll go on wanting you, but however long that is, I won't be dating anyone else. It wouldn't be fair to them."

"I...I see." And she did. Far too much. She saw that Travis had more moral fiber than she'd ever given him credit for. Maybe he didn't play by her rules, but he stuck by his own. That made him more honorable than most men she'd known.

He'd mentioned taking time to get over her before he dated someone else. She wondered if she'd ever get over him.

AS TRAVIS HELPED Gwen with the dishes, he did his damnedest to shut down his response to her. It was one of the toughest assignments he'd ever given himself.

He thought about retreating to his bedroom, but that seemed like the coward's way out and he'd never considered himself a coward. After the dishes were done, he borrowed a paperback mystery from her bookshelf. Now he was attempting to concentrate on the plot while sitting on her crushed-velvet sofa in the parlor while not five feet away she worked on her loom. She'd built a little fire in the small fireplace to take the chill off the room, so she said.

In his estimation, there was no chill in the room. Heat sizzled across the five feet separating them, and he was aware of every movement she made at the loom. He'd watched Matty weave a few times and knew the process had a steady rhythm to it. He hadn't realized that rhythm could be sexy.

As Gwen worked the treadles with her feet, his attention got snagged on the flex of her ankles, the bend in her knees, the subtle motion of her thighs.... He thought of nestling between those soft thighs and his mouth went dry. And each colorful thread was snugged into place with a soft thumping sound that made him think of...well, never mind what it made him think of.

It occurred to him that he'd never spent this kind of leisure time with a woman his own age since he hit puberty. Lovemaking, or leading up to it, or recovering from it had always been the primary activity connected with a lady friend.

Except for the heavy sexual tension in the room, he might have enjoyed the chance to be with Gwen on this quiet evening, each doing something different, yet sharing the same space. The idea intrigued him, except he was too aroused to know if he liked the concept. All he could think of was dragging Gwen off that stool and tearing her clothes off—starting his own kind of rhythm, weaving his own brand of excitement.

Whenever the pressure to do that became too intense, he went upstairs to check on Lizzie. He made quite a few trips upstairs.

He'd started up for maybe the sixth or seventh time when Lizzie started coughing. And this cough sounded different from the way she'd coughed during the day. There was a barking quality to it that he didn't like at all. He called to Gwen as he took the stairs two at a time.

She arrived in the room right after he did, which told him she'd been on her feet before he'd called her.

He scooped Lizzie up and turned to Gwen. "She's worse."

"She does sound a little croupy," Gwen admitted. "That can happen at night."

Travis fought panic. If anything happened to this kid, his life would be over. "Let's take her to the doc."

"We can do that," Gwen said, "but it's started raining out there."

"Raining?" He hadn't even noticed. That's how completely he'd been focusing on Gwen.

"It's getting sort of nasty. Could turn to sleet, I think. Let's try something before we take her out in a cold rain," Gwen said.

Travis thanked his lucky stars he wasn't out at the ranch alone with Lizzie. "What?"

"One of my guests had a kid with a cough like that. They turned on the hot water in the shower and closed themselves in there with the baby. The bathroom was almost like a sauna. It didn't do much for my wallpaper, but it worked wonders on that cough."

"Let's do it. I'll get you new wallpaper." He could feel Lizzie's cough vibrating through her little body. She was coughing so hard, he was afraid she'd shake something loose inside.

"I'll start the shower," Gwen said. Then she turned back to him. "It'll be hot and humid in there. You might want to strip her down to her diaper and take off your shirt."

"Got it." He laid Lizzie back in the crib and pulled off his shirt so fast the snaps popped like buckshot. If he hadn't been so worried, he'd have laughed. Gwen had just ordered him to take off his shirt. He'd been hoping for such a request for hours.

In seconds he had Lizzie undressed, and he carried her toward the bathroom.

Gwen came out and closed the door behind her. Her hair was damp and her blouse clung to her breasts. "It's steaming up pretty good in there. Go on in and I'll get some apple juice she can drink when you bring her out again."

"And if it doesn't help?"

"Then we'll bundle her up as best we can and go over to Doc Harrison's house. But I think this might work."

Travis looked into her eyes and drew confidence from her. "I don't want to take any chances."

"Don't worry. We won't."

His panic eased. He didn't put his trust in a lot of people, but putting his trust in Gwen felt good and right. Something shifted in the region of his heart, as if a barricade had toppled.

He gave her a swift kiss on the mouth. "That didn't count as a pass," he said. "It's just my way of saying thank you." Then he carried a coughing Lizzie into the steam-filled bathroom and closed the door.

9

ALL THE WAY DOWNSTAIRS and into the kitchen, Gwen savored Travis's "thank-you" kiss. No matter how much her mouth tingled, she now believed him to be a man of his word, and she didn't think the kiss had been any kind of seductive gesture.

He'd simply been grateful for her presence and her suggestion of the steam bath for Elizabeth's cough. It would be entirely in character for a man like him to show his gratitude with a kiss. But Travis, being Travis, couldn't give a woman a brotherly peck. He only had one mode—full out.

She poured apple juice in one of Elizabeth's bottles and secured the nipple. No, Travis wasn't about to go back on his word to stay away from her. After all, he'd sat reading a book for two hours in the same room and hadn't made a single suspicious move. She'd obviously convinced him that she didn't want him to make love to her. Damn it.

No, not damn it. Good. She didn't want to be one of those women who claimed no responsibility for sex, who allowed herself to be "swept away," and then pretended she'd been seduced against her will and was simply a victim of a man's relentless sex drive. That was operating from weakness and Gwen considered it unworthy of a modern woman.

She started back up the stairs. She might be a modern woman, but she'd had an old-fashioned reaction to Travis when he'd appeared bare-chested in the hall carrying Elizabeth a short while ago. Advertisers had been making hay recently with the image of a well-muscled father holding his tiny baby, and Gwen had thought the campaigns were overdone and trite.

But her entire take on the subject had changed when she'd emerged from the misty bathroom to discover Travis approaching with Elizabeth. She'd never seen him without a shirt before, never realized that he was truly a work of art. She'd been totally unprepared for his powerful biceps and well-developed pecs. And he had exactly the right amount of chest hair to suit her, enough to provide a tactile thrill against bare breasts, but not so much that a girl would feel as if she was making love to a furry beast.

At the sight of Travis bare-chested, she'd been swamped with unknown and unfamiliar instincts heating her blood and heightening her senses. She'd longed to bury her nose against his throat and breathe in his scent, to rake his flesh with her teeth. To stake her claim. To mate.

Ridiculous fantasies, she told herself now as she stood on the landing and watched light and steam filter from under the bathroom door. Travis had no intention of being anyone's mate. Obviously her instincts were leading her astray.

Elizabeth's barking cough came again, but it sounded looser. Gwen was no expert, but she thought the steam was having an effect. She tapped lightly on the door. "How's it going?"

"I think it's helping her," Travis called above the sound of the shower and Elizabeth's coughing. "Although your wallpaper doesn't look too good. How long do you think we should stay in here?"

"At least a few more minutes. Until the coughing slows down some more. I don't care about the wallpaper, but what about you? Are you growing webbed feet?"

In response he croaked like a frog, and she laughed. "I'll take a turn next. I brought up the apple juice."

"Good. Where will you be?"

Gwen enjoyed the feeling of being needed, if only temporarily. "I'll stay in her bedroom and wait for you."

"Okay. Don't go far."

"I won't." It was *very* nice to be needed. She walked into Elizabeth's room and switched on a bedside lamp. Then she crossed to the window and looked out.

Sure enough, the rain had turned to sleet. Summer would come eventually to the Rockies, but it hadn't arrived yet. Elizabeth shouldn't be taken out in this weather unless absolutely necessary, she decided. The cold sleet would be hard enough on her, but the streets would be treacherous, making it risky to drive even the few blocks to Doc Harrison's house.

She and Travis could handle this.

She walked over to the crib and took Elizabeth's sock monkey out. Then she set the bottle of apple juice on the dresser, went over to the double canopy bed and sat down to stare into the monkey's button eyes. Matty had bought the stuffed animal at Coogan's the day after Elizabeth had been left on Sebastian's doorstep, and it had become the baby's favorite toy.

Gwen remembered the light in Matty's eyes when she'd described Sebastian using the monkey like a puppet when he played with Elizabeth. Matty said her heart melted every time she watched Sebastian interact with Elizabeth, and now Gwen found herself in the same predicament watching Travis care for the baby. Only Gwen didn't want her heart to melt.

From the bathroom came the squeak of a faucet handle, and the sound of running water ceased. Travis must have decided Elizabeth could take a break from the steam treatment. Gwen hoped he'd think to wrap the baby in a towel when he brought her out, so she wouldn't get chilled.

"What do you think, Bruce?" Gwen propped the monkey on her lap. "Are we handling this the way Matty and Sebastian would want us to?"

"I think so," Travis said from the doorway.

Gwen looked up. He was still shirtless, of course. His skin was damp and drops of condensed steam clung to his chest. The steam had turned his hair into a cap of ringlets, making him look even sexier, if such a thing was possible. Her heart warmed as she saw that he'd bundled Elizabeth in a towel like a little papoose, with only her face sticking out. He was such a good daddy.

The baby coughed once, sticking her little tongue out in the process, but the alarming bark was nearly gone.

Travis wiped her nose with a tissue he pulled from the pocket of his jeans. "I think she's better than she was," he said, "and I think she's ready for some apple juice."

Gwen put down the monkey and held out her arms. "I'll take her. Are you cold? Maybe you should grab a towel for yourself." *Please get a towel for yourself.*

"I will. Here you go." He settled Elizabeth in her

arms, which required only minimal contact between them, the brush of his bare arm against her sleeve, a whisper of his male scent when he moved. His erect nipple passed within two inches of her mouth.

Although he didn't make a big deal out of being close to her while he was half-naked, Gwen nearly went out of her mind with the urge to kiss and nibble every inch of that tempting chest. Then she made the colossal mistake of looking into his golden eyes. Framed by lashes spiked with moisture from the steam bath, they glowed with banked passion. She gulped.

She *so* wanted this man. How sweet it would be to lift her mouth for his kiss, to beg him to make love to her until neither of them could see straight.

His gaze warmed a fraction more. Clearly he wanted her, too. All he needed was a word from her, and...

"The juice is on the dresser," she said.

"Right." He turned away from her and picked up the bottle. "Here you go," he said as he handed it to her.

"Thanks." She offered the bottle to Elizabeth, who took it greedily.

Travis cleared his throat. "That's a good sign, isn't it? Being so eager for it?" He coughed. "I meant Lizzie, with the bottle...."

"I'm sure it's a good sign." Gwen swallowed hard. If she didn't show any embarrassment over his comment, there didn't have to be any.

"Yeah, a real good sign."

"An excellent sign." She sneaked a peek at him.

He stood watching her, not the baby, and the fire in

his eyes was unmistakable. But the minute her gaze met his, he glanced away. "Weather's nasty out."

"Yes, nasty." She looked quickly back at Elizabeth. "Good thing she seems to be getting better."

"Yep, sure is."

"I'll take a turn in the sauna after she finishes her bottle," Gwen said. "Then maybe she'll sleep for a while."

"That would be good."

"Yes." Good for Elizabeth, dangerous for her, Gwen thought. When Elizabeth was asleep, she and Travis had way too much time on their hands. She became aware of his breathing in the stillness of the room. She wanted him to put something on, damn it, but to ask would give her away.

And she dared not raise her glance again. Instead she blurted out the next thing that came into her head. "Have you ever noticed that apple juice is the same color as beer?" She closed her eyes in mortification. What an idiotic thing to say. Better to endure the thick silence than babble like an imbecile.

"I can't say I ever did." He sounded as if he was seriously considering the subject. "But now that you mention it, I'll stay alert when I'm on apple juice detail, so we don't accidentally get Lizzie ploughed."

Now that she'd started this ridiculous conversational thread she decided to keep it going. "I didn't think to offer you a beer with dinner. I have some in the refrigerator, though, if you'd like to have—"

"Thanks, but I decided to forgo booze this week. No point in taking a chance of being even slightly fuzz-brained while I'm in charge of the kid, especially now, when she's sick."

"That's...that's very responsible of you."

"You sound surprised." There was an edge of irritation to his voice.

She glanced up. "Sorry. It's just that—"

"A guy like me couldn't be expected to give up his quota of beer for the week?" A mix of anger and sexual awareness lit his gaze, and he looked like an avenging god standing there. "As if a few long-necks mean a damn to me compared to Lizzie's welfare. I guess you haven't figured out yet that I'd do anything for this kid."

Gwen took a deep breath. "I apologize. I have figured that out. But you're making me nervous. I'd appreciate it if you'd go put on a shirt."

He looked confused for a minute. "A shirt?" Then understanding obviously dawned. "Oh. A *shirt*."

"Please."

He nodded. "Be right back." He started out of the room.

"Take your time. I can handle Elizabeth for a while." *But I can't handle you.*

Travis walked into his room and picked up the shirt he'd thrown across the bed. He moved slowly, taking his time as Gwen had suggested. They both needed time apart to cool off.

Doggone it, he didn't know how he was going to survive this. He'd never been in a situation like this one, where both parties wanted to make love but one of them, namely the woman, had reservations. Women had never had reservations about him before.

That was what made Gwen so special, he realized. She didn't allow herself to be ruled by her desires. *And neither did he.* The thought amazed him, but once it had popped into his head, he knew it was true. Being around Lizzie had stirred up all sorts of desires he'd tried to bury, like the urge to get married and have a family, the urge to have a place of his own and not be on the move so much, the urge to grow old with one, special woman who was *not* his mother.

But he was smart enough to know that his mother wouldn't mix well with another woman. She was as demanding as a spoiled saddle horse, as bossy as the oldest mare in the herd, as territorial as a mama cougar.

Travis's father had always given Luann everything she wanted, and the result was that she required Travis's undivided attention when he was around. She claimed to love the secluded cabin in Utah, and had said she'd never consider moving.

His commitment to his father left him with no choice but to forget marriage for the time being, and maybe for good.

Gwen wanted a husband, and he envied the lucky son-of-a-bitch who would have that privilege. She'd make somebody one hell of a wife, one hell of a lover, one hell of a mother to their children. He couldn't think about that too much or he might go a little crazy.

He was tucking in his shirt when he heard Lizzie start to cough again. He hurried into the other bedroom and nearly collided with Gwen.

"She started up again after I changed her diaper," she said. "I'm taking her back into the steam."

His stomach began to churn with anxiety as he listened to Lizzie's barking cough. "What can I do?"

"Make us some coffee," Gwen said. "I have a feeling we'll be up most of the night with her."

"Maybe it's time to call Doc Harrison."

"And take her out on those slick roads?"

He hesitated. "We could ask him to come here."

"We could, and we will, if the steam treatments stop working. But I've watched parents go through this when they've been unlucky enough to have a kid get sick on vacation here at Hawthorne House. They've told me it's usually a matter of accepting that you'll have a sleepless night and keeping watch. Waiting it out, basically."

"I hate her being sick. I can deal with anything else, but this is the pits."

"I know." Gwen's smile was determined. "Welcome to parenthood."

He made a face. "I'll bet this is the part that makes you old and gray before your time. I'll go make the coffee." He headed down the stairs. Behind him the bathroom door closed and the water came on.

Lizzie would help keep him in check where Gwen was concerned, he thought as he started making the coffee, but he'd trade a thousand frustrating nights with Gwen in exchange for Lizzie being well. If she turned even slightly worse, he was calling Doc Harrison and telling him to get his butt over here.

TRAVIS NEVER DID call the doctor, although he came close two or three times. But finally, about four in the morning, Lizzie seemed to be over the hump. She felt cooler to his now-experienced touch, and her cough didn't come nearly as often. Best of all, it was a normal cough, and not the harsh croupy one he'd learned to hate the sound of.

"Let's see what happens if we put her down for a while." Gwen carried a drowsy Lizzie over to the crib and laid her gently on her tummy.

The baby's eyelids fluttered and closed. Her breathing seemed almost normal.

"Thank God," Travis murmured as he stood by the crib. His nerves were strung tight with worry and too much caffeine.

"I think we made it," Gwen said. "Let's sneak out and see if she stays asleep."

"Go ahead. I'm gonna watch a little longer and make sure she doesn't start up again." He'd lost count of the number of times they'd left the room and started down the stairs, only to turn right around when Lizzie had started coughing. They'd taken turns with the steam in the bathroom, and the wallpaper seams had all begun to curl from the constant moisture.

Travis felt a little like a swamp creature, himself, although he'd been careful to put his shirt back on each time after Gwen had reminded him about it. She'd stayed dressed, of course, and each time she'd come out of the steamy bathroom with her blouse plastered to her breasts, he'd had to turn away and get control of himself.

"Do you want any more coffee?" she whispered softly from the doorway.

"God, no. I think I'll be awake for a week as it is."

"I could brew some chamomile tea."

He glanced at her standing in the doorway, wanting to help, and gratitude softened his response. "Thanks, but I'm not really into the herbal tea scene."

She smiled. "Hot chocolate?"

"Maybe." God, she was beautiful. The steam had taken all the curl out of her hair, and it spilled over her shoulders and down to the sweet rise of her breasts in one smooth river of black. He knew what he wanted from her, and it sure wasn't hot chocolate. "Let's see if she stays asleep."

"I'll be downstairs."

He watched her go, his body aching with the need to hold her. He'd just have to get over it.

WITH EVERY STEP Gwen took down the stairs away from Travis, she became more sure that she would make love to him. That is, if he would have her, and she thought there was a good chance he would.

Watching his tireless dedication to Elizabeth through the long hours of the night had worn away the last of her resistance and replaced it with admiration. She was lucky enough to have a rare and wonderful man under her roof, and she'd be a fool to miss the opportunity he offered.

He'd told her he couldn't give her more than pleasure. She no longer believed him. She'd seen the depth of his character tonight, his capacity for patience, courage...and love. If he could give of himself to a child, he could do the same with a woman, the right woman.

Gwen believed she was the right woman. People so often gave to others what they wished for themselves. Because she'd been with Travis through this harrowing crisis with the baby, she knew something about Travis that no other woman did. She knew what he wished for, even if he didn't know it himself.

Carefully she prepared the hot chocolate...and waited.

IF HE HAD any sense, he'd stay upstairs, Travis thought. He could lie on that frilly canopy bed for a while. Even if he was too wired to sleep, he could try and get some rest. Ha. Rest was out of the question with Gwen in the house.

As of this moment, making love to her seemed like the only thing in the world worth doing. He wondered if that was a normal reaction parents had after going through a night of worry over a kid. What a comfort that would be, to turn to each other and celebrate making it through the ordeal.

He thought they had made it through. For the first time since yesterday Lizzie's cheeks weren't flushed deep rose. Instead they were a soft, healthy pink. He stood by the crib listening to her steady breathing and the knot in his gut loosened. Yes, she was better, really better. Earlier he'd only been hoping she was better, but now he knew, in the same way he knew when he'd finally made the exact right adjustment on the carburetor of his truck.

He'd had to go through this whole night constantly gauging her condition to become an expert, but now he was one. He knew something about taking care of Lizzie that Matty and Sebastian didn't know. That made him feel pretty damn good. Wonderful, in fact.

His step was light as he walked down the stairs and into the kitchen.

Gwen stood at the stove, her back to him as she stirred what smelled like hot chocolate in a pan on the stove. Steam rose from the pan.

"Lizzie's better," he announced happily. "I'm sure of it."

Gwen switched off the burner and turned, a smile on her face.

Her smile knocked him for a loop, and he couldn't have explained why if somebody had held a gun to his head. All he knew was that he wanted her so much it was making him dizzy. He didn't dare say anything as he waited for the feeling to pass. Maybe he'd hurt women before, like she'd said, but he damned sure wasn't going to hurt her.

Her lips moved, but he couldn't hear her with the buzzing in his ears. She walked toward him with the most amazing light in her eyes, and then she laid both hands flat against his chest.

His voice sounded hoarse, as if he'd been the one who'd been sick. "Gwen, I don't think you'd better—"

"I do." She slid her hands around his neck and kissed him.

10

HE WAS IRRESISTIBLE. Gwen could no more have
stopped herself from walking over and kissing Travis
than she could have stopped herself from breathing.
As he stood there glowing with happiness because the
little baby they'd spent the night tending was finally
better, his uncomplicated joy captured her as nothing
else could have.

She'd barely touched her mouth to his before he
took her by the shoulders and eased her away from
him. "Hey," he muttered, his breath coming fast.
"Watch that. I know you feel happy about this. So do
I, but—"

"I feel grateful," she said in a husky voice.

"Yeah, me, too. But the thing is, I'm not in very
good control of myself right now."

"I feel *very* grateful." She was desperate to be near
him, to touch the essence that was Travis. She tried to
close the distance between them.

His grip tightened as he kept her from moving
closer, and his voice roughened. "I know. I'm grateful,
too, but if you kiss me, stuff's gonna happen."

"Yes." She focused on the point where his fingers
clutched her shoulders and imagined his touch over
her entire naked body. Oh, yes.

His gaze grew hot. "Damn it, Gwen, this isn't a
game."

"No."

He searched her face, as if trying to understand. "You want to..."

"Yes."

"Why?"

She trembled with desire. "I told you. I'm grateful. Grateful that such a good man is standing in my kitchen."

Conflicting emotions burned in his eyes—passion and restraint fighting it out. "I'm not a good man. You were right. I use pleasure to get women to agree to my rules. It's not fair."

She took a long, shuddering breath. "You'll give me more than just pleasure."

Wariness crept into his golden gaze. "I can't—"

"Yes, you will." She looked past his hesitation and found raw hunger, the kind only she could satisfy. "And I won't ask for promises, but I know who you are, Travis. I know what you need."

He closed his eyes and groaned softly. "You don't know. Don't do this. You'll get hurt."

"After watching you with Lizzie tonight, I'm willing to take that chance." She cupped his beard-stubbled face in both hands. "Come to bed with me," she whispered.

His body shuddered in reaction as he stood, eyes closed, head bowed. Finally he released her shoulders to cup his hands over hers. Then he brought her palm up to his mouth and kissed her tenderly there.

Her pulse raced as she waited for his answer, although she was sure what it would be. He was, after all, a highly sexed man. And he'd finally heard the invitation he'd been wanting since the wedding. He wouldn't be able to resist her any more than she could resist him. And she would show him what love could be.

But when he opened his eyes, his gaze was bleak and his voice was tight. "No." He cleared his throat. "I can't believe I'm saying this, but no." Giving her hands a squeeze he released her and stepped back.

The unexpected rejection cut through her, leaving her breathless with pain. She should turn away while she could still maintain some composure. "Why?"

"Because I care about you too much."

She saw the light burning in his eyes and knew he'd told her the truth, a truth that wiped away her pain. A truth that gave her hope. "I see."

He backed toward the door leading into the hall. "This is for the best."

"Maybe it is." She pressed her lips together to keep from smiling.

"I'll...go on upstairs, then."

She nodded.

"Are you...are you okay?"

She nodded again. "Fine." Then she realized that sounded too carefree. "Disappointed, but I'm sure I'll get over it."

"Good." He looked positively miserable as he turned and walked down the hall. His steps as he climbed the stairs sounded like the tread of a doomed man.

Which he was, she thought with a grin as she hurried into her bedroom. A quick shower, some scented lotion, a dab of cologne at various strategic spots, and she was ready. A red silk robe that would slide off her shoulders and pool at her feet provided the dramatic touch she was looking for. Then she dug through her

vanity for the foil packages a guest had left behind
and slipped them in the pocket of her robe.

Her skin flushed with anticipation, she turned off
the lights and started up the stairs.

LISTENING TO the shower going downstairs, Travis
suffered the agony of imagining Gwen with water
rushing over her sweet body. He tried to think of other
things to distract himself.

He'd mentally ridden every mile of barbed-wire
fence on both Matty's and Sebastian's spreads. Staring
out through the lace curtains covering the double-
hung bedroom window, he'd watched the raindrops
hit the glass and relived last year's roundup, complete
with the cold rain that had made the experience one of
his least favorites in the Rockies.

But thinking of the rain brought him back around to
the shower running downstairs, and Gwen standing
naked under it. Sure enough, he started wondering
what color her nipples were. From her Native American ancestry he imagined them dusky-rose against her
honey-shaded skin.

If the shower was warm and the pressure light,
they'd be petal soft and supple to the touch, velvety
under a man's fingers. But if she'd adjusted the spray
to pelt her breasts and cooled the temperature of the
water to draw the heat of desire from her body, her
nipples would be taut and nubby, ready for the curl of
a man's tongue and the nip of a man's teeth.

He licked dry lips and wished...oh, hell. Now he
was lying in her tidy little guest room with an erection
so hard he could chip stone with it. He'd never be able
to sleep in that condition, but then he hadn't much expected to sleep, anyway. Getting out of that kitchen

without grabbing Gwen had been the biggest achieve-
ment of his sorry life. Once finding the strength to do
that, he now had to meet the challenge of staying
where he was until daybreak.

He had no business going downstairs for many reasons, but one compelling one was the lack of birth control. Because he'd promised not to touch her if she'd
let him stay with Lizzie, he hadn't brought any with
him when he'd come back to Hawthorne House from
the ranch. She probably hadn't thought of preventing
pregnancy when she invited him to share her bed. He
hadn't thought of it, either, but he did now.

Of course, they could have made love in other ways,
bypassing the need for condoms and still staying safe.
He could imagine how she'd taste, and how her
mouth would feel on him. Oh, they could have a fine
time, even without birth control. But that was neither
here nor there, because he was staying upstairs. He
most certainly was.

Daybreak. He could last until then. Once the sun
came up he could cart Lizzie over to Doc Harrison's
for another quick check before he took her back out to
the ranch. He could handle things on his own, now
that the immediate danger was past. Yep, all he had to
do was make it to daybreak.

And he would make it, somehow. Sure he would.
Staying up here and out of her bed was the right thing
to do for Gwen, and for himself, too. Making love to
her would have landed them both in hot water. He already felt a mental connection to her that was different from what he'd felt for any other women. Add a
sexual relationship and no telling what sort of mess
he'd get into.

He turned away from the window and shifted to his

back. The smooth sheet caressed his stiffened penis. Damn. Maybe he shouldn't have stripped all the way down before climbing into this bed, but he'd always preferred sleeping in the raw and had followed his usual pattern. He hadn't been alone in bed with an erection since he was fifteen.

And he'd had a method for taking care of the situation when he was fifteen, he thought with a grimace. He'd hoped not to be reduced to such measures ever again, but this problem was bordering on painful. A cold shower was out for him. He didn't want to take the chance of waking Lizzie by running water so close to her room.

Ah, he was in agony. The family jewels ached almost as much as if he'd been kicked. And no telling how long the condition would last. He couldn't very well walk into Doc Harrison's office in such a state, that was for sure.

Unfortunately, only one solution seemed available to give him relief, and he felt like a teenager having to resort to it, but he had no choice. With a sigh of resignation he threw back the covers and wrapped his fingers around the solid shaft. Squeezing the sensitive tip, he moaned. He would have rather had Gwen's soft hand caressing him right there instead of his own callused one, but the price was too high.

He closed his eyes and tried to imagine Gwen there with him. As he started a slow stroke upward, the loose board on the stairs creaked.

He stopped in mid-motion, his heart hammering. She was probably coming up to check on the baby. He lay there, his jaw clenched, his penis hot and straining in his grip as he waited to hear the stair creak again, signaling that she'd gone back to her room.

Instead the door edged open.

A night light in the hall threw her into silhouette, but he knew the bed was still in deep shadow. She wouldn't be able to see him until her eyes adjusted to the darkness.

Her scent beckoned to him, an erotic combination of perfumed soap, her cologne, and aroused woman. His body twitched in response. Slowly he unclenched his fingers from around his shaft and eased his hand to his side. He dared not move much. Maybe she was only checking to make sure he was asleep. Maybe...

Then he almost stopped breathing. Gliding as quietly as a ghost, she stepped into the room and closed the door silently behind her. Bare feet whispered over the Oriental carpet as she crossed to the bed, bringing that wonderful aroma with her.

"Are you asleep?" she whispered.

If he hadn't been so damned aroused he might have laughed at that. He wondered if he'd even be able to speak around the knot in his vocal cords. "No." He sounded like a rusty hinge. "Is...Lizzie okay?"

"Yes."

"Good." In the dim light from the window he could make out that she wore some sort of soft bathrobe that tied around the waist. He could only think of one reason why she'd come into his room, and God help him, he no longer had the strength to send her away.

"I can't see you very well," she said.

"That's good." He decided to wait and not make a move, in case he was wrong.

"Why?" she asked softly.

"You'd probably be shocked."

Her voice dropped to a low, sensual purr. "Because you're lying there naked?"

"There's that." His body hummed and throbbed, demanding release.

Her breathing quickened. "And...hard?"

"That, too."

She untied her robe and lifted it from her shoulders. "Maybe I can help." As she lowered her arms, the robe drifted to the floor.

He swallowed. Even in the dim light from the window, he could tell she was magnificent. Her breasts were as full as he'd imagined and her nipples tipped up slightly, as if in invitation to his eager mouth. Her narrow waist flared to graceful hips and thighs perfectly made to cradle a man...or birth a child. And that was exactly the kind of notion that would get him in trouble.

"That is if you'll let me help," she added, her tone sultry. "Or are you going to send me away in some noble gesture?"

"No one's that noble, Gwen."

She stepped close to the bed and gazed down at him. "I want the light."

"So do I." He propped himself up on one elbow and reached for the bedside lamp switch.

"Wait." She rounded the bed and walked to the window.

He kept his thumb on the switch as she reached up to pull down the rolled shade. When she raised her arm, he sucked in a breath at the beauty of her in profile against the silver light from the window. Then she pulled the shade and he shoved his thumb against the switch, blinking furiously so he wouldn't miss that first, revealing moment.

"Oo. Bright light." She brought her hand up to her eyes to protect them.

"Ah, Gwen." He sighed with pleasure as his gaze traveled from the curve of her throat down the valley between her breasts, over the sweet indentation of her navel, and finally to the dark curls covering her sex.

She peeked through her fingers at him, and a slow smile curved her full mouth. "Ah, *Travis.*" She lowered her hand and glanced boldly at his arousal. "Were you expecting me?"

"No. Wishful thinking." His breathing grew ragged. "Listen, you need to know that I don't have any—"

"I do. In the pocket of my robe."

He gazed at her and shook his head in wonder. "I must be dreaming."

"Sometimes dreams come true." She put a knee on the bed and leaned toward him. Her breasts swayed gently as she moved.

"I've never dreamed anything this terrific."

"I know. Me, either." She leaned down to brush her lips against his.

"If this is a dream—" he paused and slid a hand under her hair, spreading his fingers to cup the back of her head "—don't wake me."

"I only plan to love you," she murmured. Then she settled her lips against his.

Her kiss nearly made him erupt. He had no idea a woman could suggest so much with a kiss, but Gwen was telling him with the movement of her lips and tongue exactly what was on her mind. He groaned and thrust his tongue deep, telling her exactly what was on his.

She drew back a fraction, and her sweet breath feathered his mouth as she whispered the word *soon.*

He sure hoped so. They'd spent hours in mental foreplay, and he was beyond ready.

He cupped the weight of her breast, and a tremor of need shook him. "Lie back," he urged softly. "I want—"

"Not yet." She wrapped her fingers around his shaft, as he'd imagined her doing only moments ago, when he'd been alone.

And just like that, she was in complete charge. He had all he could do to keep sane as she stroked him with loving care. *Loving.* It was the only word that stayed in his fevered mind as she leaned down to caress him with her tongue, her lips, her breath, even the silken strands of her hair.

He didn't think he could last...and yet he wanted this to go on forever. He'd never felt so cherished by a lover before, so aware of the gift...or the giver. He groaned her name and bunched her hair in his fist as he fought for control. When he thought he'd lose the battle, she paused, as if knowing she dare not push him any further.

"There." Her voice was soft and rich with satisfaction.

Gulping for air, he opened his fist and let her hair slide through his fingers as she moved up beside him. He looked into her dark eyes. He'd seen passion many times in a lover's gaze. He'd seen urgency and need. He'd never seen unconditional love. Until now.

He could almost hear the crash of barriers coming down as he drank in the emotion like a man dying of thirst. The drive to possess this woman rose in him, making him quiver with the force of it. He needed to be cradled by those soft thighs, to be deep within her loving, giving body.

Understanding flickered in her eyes and her lips parted slightly, symbolically. A red haze blurred his vision. He'd never wanted a woman this much. Never. He rolled her to her back and moved between her thighs.

She murmured something, but desire had deafened him to everything but satisfying this incredible need for her. For Gwen. For her warm body, her heat, her moist, silken sheath to enfold him. He prepared to thrust deep.

"Travis!" she whispered hoarsely, pushing at his chest. "Wait."

And only then did he realize what he'd been about to do.

Muttering a soft oath, he drew back. "Gwen, I'm sorry." He leaned his forehead against hers, his breathing ragged. "I don't know what I was thinking."

Her voice was low and heavy with desire. "Don't you?"

He lifted his head to look into her eyes. He could drown in those deep brown eyes. And he wanted to sink into her, now, without any barriers between them. He must be going crazy. "What...do you mean?"

"You want a baby."

"No." He ran from the truth as fast as he could go. "I want you. And I lost control."

She gazed at him with those knowing, passion-filled eyes.

He took a shaky breath. "But I'm back in control."

"Are you?"

She was getting way too close to his secrets, he decided. Time to distract her, and with luck, himself.

"Oh, yes. Back in control." He leaned down and placed a kiss in the hollow of her throat. He'd been meaning to make this journey, anyway. Now was the time.

Easing farther down on the bed, he scooped the weight of her breast into his cupped hand and flicked his tongue over her nipple. Ah, heaven. When he drew her into his mouth, her whimper of delight told him she might not object to a little of the attention she'd lavished on him.

Loving her was sweet torture. Every inch of her skin begged to be explored, to be licked and nuzzled and kissed. Again, and yet again. But every new exploration ratcheted his own tension up another notch.

Still, it was only fair that he should steal her sanity the way she'd stolen his, and he loved knowing he was doing that. Her quivering sighs became sharp gasps, and when at last he parted her thighs to taste her womanhood, she whispered his name and trembled uncontrollably in his arms. And he knew that he'd been granted a privilege, being allowed to touch her this way.

Only the luckiest man in the world would be allowed to bestow this intimate, erotic kiss and listen to her soft moans as he moved his tongue in a gentle, insistent rhythm. He was that man. And he wanted... yes, he wanted to be that man forever. And he could not be.

Frustration poured through his mind like lava, bringing greater urgency to his caress. He'd meant to excite, to tease, to stop short of taking her over the edge. Now he didn't want to stop. He needed her to surrender everything now, when she was most vulnerable, most open to the caress of his lips and tongue, as if that would seal some sort of pact.

It made no logical sense, but logic wasn't what drove him. She thrashed under him and at last arched upward, pleading for release.

Fiercely he gave it, absorbing her shudders. His body throbbed in response and nearly followed her into the whirlwind. She was his. *His.*

She muffled her cries with a pillow as she bucked in his arms. Finally she grew still and sagged weakly in his arms. He eased her back against the mattress.

He had no idea how he found the condoms in the pocket of her robe on the floor, or how he managed to put one on while he was shaking so violently, but somehow he managed. She lay limp and unresisting beneath him, looking up at him with those incredible eyes.

Feeling bathed in the glow of that gaze, he slid both hands under her bottom, lifted and thrust deep. Once, twice, three times, and he exploded. And then he closed his eyes, needing, for that moment, to hide.

Because she was right. He wanted a child. With her. Only with her.

11

GWEN WOKE in the dim room and noticed daylight edging the shade covering the window. The bed was empty.

For one terrible moment she was afraid Travis might have packed up Elizabeth and left, but then laughter filtered up the stairs—deep, masculine enjoyment and baby giggles. And the aroma of coffee filled the house. Gwen stretched and smiled. Still here.

She got out of bed and put on the robe that Travis had left draped across a chair. Nice of him to take time to pick up her clothes, she thought. He'd be a handy man to have around. And she believed he would be around. Only hours before, when he'd been about to make love to her, when he'd been so aroused he'd forgotten all about using protection, he'd given her *The Look*.

Gwen had waited since puberty for a look like that from the male of the species, and now that a man had given her one, she wasn't letting him blather on about staying single. When a man gave a woman *The Look*, he didn't really want to continue his bachelor life, no matter how much he insisted that he did.

She ran her fingers through her hair and headed downstairs, eager to see Travis and Elizabeth again. Yet when she came to the loose board on the stair, she stepped over it so she wouldn't make noise. She wasn't really sneaking up on Travis, she told herself.

Well, okay, she was sneaking up on him. He might try to present his carefree bachelor mask to her this morning, even though she'd seen the real Travis when they were making love. He was always real when he interacted with Elizabeth, and glimpsing him that way would give Gwen the courage to say what needed to be said.

She padded quietly to the doorway of the kitchen and peeked in. Travis had pulled on jeans and a shirt before coming downstairs, but his feet were bare. He sat in one of the oak kitchen chairs with his back to her.

Such a broad, beautiful back, she thought. Powerful and strong. Yet the nape of his neck looked so vulnerable, with the tender way his hair wanted to curl right there. His barber must have a tricky time trimming that part. She longed to put her lips against that spot, to swirl her tongue in the same pattern that the hair grew.

Travis had obviously been into the cinnamon rolls, judging from the crumb-filled pan on the table next to him. Beside it sat an empty bottle of Elizabeth's formula and a box of tissues. He had the baby propped on his left thigh and Barney the purple dinosaur propped on his right.

Apparently he was talking for the dinosaur. "You scared the spit out of us last night, Lizzie," Travis said in a Barney voice as he waggled the dinosaur's head. "Sounded like a toad in the riverbed, girl. Ribbit, ribbit."

The baby laughed and held out both chubby hands

toward the dinosaur. Then she coughed, but it was a mild cough, nothing like the night before.

"Whoops, snot alert," Travis said. He set the dinosaur on the floor and grabbed a tissue from the box.

Elizabeth strained backward against his arm, obviously trying to avoid the tissue. Gwen imagined her little pink nose was still sore.

"Gotta do this, Lizzie." Travis cupped her head and held her still while he wiped very carefully. "Otherwise you'll have green slime running down your face, and that's not gonna attract the guys, let me tell you."

Gwen smiled, but his tenderness and gentle voice had begun to affect her in more potent ways, making her skin tingle and her body quicken. She became very aware of her nakedness under the red silk as her erect nipples pushed against the material.

Travis would notice that right away. She might feel confident of the eventual outcome of their relationship, but she didn't want to be quite that obvious first thing in the morning.

She backed away from the doorway to collect herself and ran into the spindly-legged antique table she kept in the hall. The crystal dish of potpourri on top crashed to the floor and broke, scattering dried rose petals everywhere.

Embarrassed beyond belief, Gwen dropped carefully to her knees and picked up the two biggest pieces of the dish.

"Gwen? Are you okay?"

She glanced up to find him standing in the kitchen doorway, Elizabeth in his arms. Despite her embarrassment, she couldn't help enjoying the picture he made. He hadn't shaved yet, and he looked wonderfully domestic and sexy with that baby in his arms, like a daddy who had gallantly taken on the child care to give mommy more time to sleep. Oh, he would do just fine.

"I'm okay. I just bumped into the table," she said. "It's probably a dumb place to have a table like that, anyway. I think I'll put it somewhere else from now on." She stood, hoping he'd think she'd bumped into the darn thing on the way into the kitchen.

He surveyed the situation and quite obviously noticed that she was positioned between him and the mess, which meant she must have hit the table going backward. His cocksure grin flashed. "Spying on me, were you?"

"Not exactly." Heat suffused her cheeks.

He turned to the baby. "Count on it, Lizzie. She was spying. Can't say as I blame her. She's really hot for me."

Elizabeth crowed and bounced in his arms.

Gwen automatically bristled at his cavalier attitude, the very one she'd been afraid he'd show up with this morning. Eventually he'd be wonderful, but he still had a ways to go. "I'm surprised you and that ego of yours can even fit through a doorway, Evans."

"Am I wrong?"

She looked into his eyes, those golden eyes that had mesmerized her so completely a few hours ago. The gleam of male satisfaction was firmly in place. Before they'd made love, she wouldn't have looked beyond his bravado. But this morning she gazed at him a little longer and found, buried under that bluster, the shadow of uncertainty, the hunger he so rarely allowed anyone to see.

She knew how she was supposed to respond in order to play the game by his rules. She should laugh and assure him that he wasn't bad for a broken-down saddle tramp. Instead she gave him a long, steady look. "No, you're not wrong," she said softly. "I'm crazy about you."

The cocky grin slipped a little.

"I'll be even more specific than that," she continued. "I think we're meant for each other."

That wiped the smile completely off his face. "Hold on, Gwen. Don't go getting serious on me."

"Too late. I'm in for the long haul."

He stared at her, his jaw slack.

"And if you're honest with yourself, so are you. We belong together, Travis."

"Gwen, just because we had a great time in that bed upstairs doesn't mean that—"

Elizabeth grabbed his nose in her tiny fingers and twisted.

He winced and firmly removed her hand. Then he shook it gently. "Hey, Lizzie. I've already got one woman here trying to put a ring through my nose. Don't you start."

Gwen kept a tight rein on her temper. "I'm not basing this conclusion on good sex alone."

"Great sex," he corrected, glancing at her as he hoisted the baby higher up on his shoulder. "But that still doesn't mean it's white-lace-and-promises time. I warned you I wasn't into that. And don't forget that you came to my room, not the other way around. I didn't talk you into a damn thing."

"My memory of our time in bed together is perfectly good." She made sure he was looking at her before she ran her tongue deliberately over her lips. "How's yours?"

His eyes darkened. Then his gaze traveled from her

mouth to her breasts and lingered there. By the time he looked into her eyes again, his breathing was ragged. "Time to change the munchkin's diaper," he said hoarsely.

She felt no sense of triumph that she could sway him with the power of suggestion. After all, he affected her as strongly as she affected him. The only difference was that she had admitted what that meant to both of them. He was still fighting it.

"Let me sweep the hall before you walk through," she said. "I don't want you to cut your feet on a piece of glass."

"Thanks." He stepped aside and she moved past him, the silk robe swishing against her legs as she walked. She heard him gulp.

After dumping the broken halves of the dish in the garbage, she took out a broom and dustpan from the cleaning closet and walked past him again to sweep the hall.

Elizabeth gurgled and cooed in his arms, but he stayed darkly silent. Gwen was sure he was watching her every movement. And if the front of her robe happened to gape open a bit while she was leaning over to sweep the rose petals into the dust pan, she couldn't help that.

"All clear," she said at last. "While you're changing her, I think I'll go take a shower."

"Fine."

She sneaked a peek at him as he stalked out, and noticed the denim crotch of his jeans was bulging. Well, good, because she wanted him just as much.

But it wasn't only about sex, she thought as she went into her suite of rooms and took off the bathrobe. She tossed it on her bed, went into her Victorian bathroom and turned the porcelain knobs to start her shower.

She hadn't gone to Travis's room last night just because she'd wanted him sexually, although that had been part of it. She'd gone because she'd finally seen the warm and caring person under that playboy exterior he was so proud of. She'd gone because the man Travis had shown himself to be through the long night of nursing Elizabeth was a man worth loving.

He hadn't disappointed her. She'd never felt more complete than she had in Travis's arms. From his response, she knew he felt the same way. But something was keeping him from honoring that part of himself that could love, honor and cherish a woman for a lifetime. Gwen intended to find out what that something was.

In the meantime, she'd freshen up with a shower. Although she sometimes indulged in a long soak in her claw-foot tub, she'd also installed a shower head over it and hung a curtain around it for those occasions when she didn't have time for a bath.

Now was one of those times. She wound her hair on top of her head and secured it with a butterfly clip. Then she climbed into the tub, pulled the curtain into place and stepped under the warm spray. She didn't intend to linger, but the spray felt good on her skin, and she stood and let it pulse down on her. She should get going, she told herself. She needed a cup of coffee and a little breakfast. She needed—

The shower curtain whooshed back.

"Travis!" Before she could react, he wrapped his arms around her waist and lifted her out of the tub in one swift motion.

"You're driving me crazy," he muttered in her ear

as he pressed his naked, aroused body up against her slick backside.

Hot desire roared through her and she started to turn toward him, but he held her fast, cupping her breast with one hand as he slid the other boldly between her thighs.

"Where's—" She gasped as he found the sensitive nub buried deep in her curls. "Where's the baby?"

His voice rasped in her ear. "She's fine. She's in the crib, playing with Bruce."

His probing fingers had reduced her to a liquid state already, but she wasn't sure they should be doing this, with Elizabeth still awake upstairs. She tried to say that, tried to ignore the ache building in her womb, the trembling in her thighs. If he hadn't been holding her up, she would have crumpled to the floor, weak with passion. "Travis, I don't think—"

"Don't worry," he said gruffly. He continued to caress her intimately as he guided her to her knees on the fluffy rose-colored bath rug. "This won't take long."

Her heart raced as his mouth touched her damp shoulder and his teeth nipped her skin. His stroked her with knowing fingers, bringing her close, very close. And as he wooed her with his touch, he pressed his chest against her back, urging her down on all fours. He meant to take her like that, she realized, maybe so he could satisfy his lust without looking into her eyes, without allowing her to look into his. This time he didn't want her to see the emotions there.

Her mind told her to protest, but her body and soul craved the joining that he silently promised, the chance to have him deep inside her again. She welcomed his first thrust with a shudder of delight.

He groaned and thrust again. And again. His body quivered against hers with each penetration, and the heavy sound of his breathing filled the small room.

"Coward," she taunted fiercely, even as she yearned for each deliberate stroke. Her body tightened, reached, lifted.

"Witch," he said with a gasp as he drove deep.

Contractions swept through her, forcing a cry from her throat.

He increased the pace, his thighs slapping hers as the wild friction prolonged the intensity beyond anything she'd ever known. At last, when she thought he'd drive her insane with pleasure, he pushed deep, his body pulsing with release as he gasped out her name.

As he quieted, he gradually eased them both down so she lay in the circle of his body, spoon fashion, with her head pillowed on his outstretched arm.

He tenderly kissed the nape of her neck.

With that single gesture, he made her feel cherished. "I know I mean something to you," she said softly. "More than just a summer fling. I can't be wrong about that."

He smoothed a hand over the curve of her shoulder. His voice was husky. "You're not wrong. You've turned everything upside down for me. But the thing is, I can't get hooked up with you...or anyone."

She took a shaky breath. "Why not?"

He didn't respond.

"I think I deserve to know."

"Maybe you do."

"Will you tell me?"

He eased away from her. "I'll think about it." With

a final kiss on her shoulder, he got up and left the bathroom.

Eyes closed, she lay on the soft rug, her body richly satisfied, her mind in turmoil. He hadn't said he *wouldn't* commit to her. He'd said he *couldn't*. And that sounded like a more serious hurdle than she'd anticipated.

JUST LIKE he'd been afraid of, the situation was out of control. As Travis dressed and got Lizzie ready to haul her over to Doc Harrison's for a checkup, he thought how desperate he'd been when he'd gone downstairs to satisfy his unbelievable hunger for Gwen. He'd never felt like that, like some caveman who was ready to drag his mate off by her hair. It was a damn good thing Gwen had wanted to make love, because he trembled to think what he would have done if she'd refused him.

But she hadn't refused him, because she loved him. He knew it and she knew it. What's more, he was beginning to believe he was in love, too, for the first time in his life. The sexual craving, heavy-duty though it might be, wasn't his major clue, either. No, the other major clue was the kind of man he became when he was with her—a better man, a kinder man, a man he liked looking at when he shaved in the morning.

Gwen wasn't so much interested in what she could get as what she could give, and that was a novelty he didn't have much experience with. No question about it, she'd knocked him for a loop. And now he had to decide whether to tell her about his mother.

He put on his suede jacket, bundled Lizzie up and carried her downstairs. Gwen was in the kitchen making soup, and it smelled terrific. She had on a green velvet lounging outfit—pants and a long-tailed shirt. Her hair was piled on top of her head. He wanted to take down her hair and strip off her clothes.

She glanced up from the pot simmering on the stove and stopped stirring the contents. There was a question in her dark eyes.

He picked up the infant seat he'd left on one of the kitchen chairs. "I'm taking Lizzie to Doc Harrison's, to be on the safe side."

She lifted the spoon out of the pot and laid it on a spoon rest before turning toward him. "Will you be back?" Her voice cracked slightly. Obviously the answer was very important to her.

Oh, yes. He couldn't stay away, and that was what had him tied in knots. If the doc agreed that Lizzie was better, he had no excuse to stay with Gwen another night, but that's all he could think about. "We'll be back."

The tense lines around her eyes relaxed. "Good. We need to talk."

"I know." He felt Lizzie slipping and hoisted her up more firmly against his shoulder. The baby gurgled and grabbed for his ear. With one hand holding the infant seat and the other holding the infant, he couldn't do anything about it while she twisted the lobe of his ear in her baby fingers.

"Hey, Elizabeth, don't be so rough." Gwen stepped closer, reached up and unclenched the baby's fingers. Then she offered her own finger for Lizzie to hold, and there they were, all linked together.

He breathed in Gwen's scent and grew dizzy from wanting her. When he spoke, his voice was tight. "As long as I'm going out, do you need anything?"

Pink tinged her cheeks, and she had that look in her

eyes, the one that made him feel about ten feet tall. "Only for you to come back," she said.

"I will. This won't take long."

Her color deepened, and he realized he'd said exactly the same thing right before he'd made love to her beside her claw-foot tub. Damn, he was aroused in no time thinking of the way she'd opened to him, the way she'd cried out, the way he'd felt at the moment of climax.

He looked into her eyes and was sure she was reliving it, too, by the fire in her gaze and the quickening of her breath. He cleared his throat. "I need to go. Lizzie's getting hot."

Gwen smiled at that and slipped her finger out of the baby's grip. "I'll bet."

"See you soon." He left the kitchen while he could still walk. What a mess, he thought as he went out the front door into the rain-dampened morning. Gwen was the ruler of her pretty Victorian house, and his mother ruled the cabin tucked into the forest in Utah. Unfortunately, he couldn't imagine either of them giving up their kingdoms.

12

ONCE TRAVIS WAS GONE Gwen pulled on a light trench coat and went for a walk around her tidy little neighborhood. She'd been cooped up too long in the house and the fresh air would help her think. The minute she stepped out on her front porch and breathed in the pine scent of the blue spruce in her front yard, she knew she'd made the right decision.

The morning breeze was brisk but the sun warmed the wet grass and the sidewalk was already beginning to dry. Everywhere she looked were signs of spring— trees budding, birds chirping and tulip and daffodil bulbs sending shoots up through the damp earth in the neat flower beds that trimmed nearly every home. Snow might still drape the Sangre de Cristo Mountains, but the valley would soon overflow with blooming color.

No doubt about it, she loved this place. She'd made it a point to meet her neighbors so that she could call out a greeting whenever she saw them. At Christmas she took home-baked goodies to each of the houses on her block, and Halloween meant giving all her little friends treats as they proudly showed off their costumes.

She'd grieved with elderly Mrs. Jackson over her dearly departed cat, and given weaving lessons to ten-year-old Lisa Henry. She'd baby-sat for the Johnsons when the young couple had desperately needed a night away, and she'd taken soup to Ethel Sweetwater when she'd come down with the flu. Her neighbors automatically included her in family celebrations and happily spread the word about her bed and breakfast, bringing her more guests every year.

For the first time Gwen began to wonder how loving Travis might change all that. He had a winter home in Utah, but he traveled to Colorado every summer to work for Matty. Now he'd be working for Matty and Sebastian. Assuming she could overcome whatever obstacle was keeping him from a commitment, would he expect her to live in Utah and only spend summers here, like a tourist? Could she uproot herself after so carefully and painstakingly making the little town of Huerfano her home?

Huerfano meant *orphan* in Spanish according to her brother, who'd said it was a melancholy name for a town. Gwen had always liked it. She thought of this place as a haven for anyone who felt orphaned, which she had, in a way, despite having parents. To her, an orphan was someone who had no real home, no place where they belonged, and until she'd moved to Huerfano, she'd felt like that.

She hoped that Travis's place in Utah wasn't anything special to him. With luck it was a typical bachelor's hangout, with no real character. He liked her house. She could tell by the way he'd made himself so completely at home.

And at home with the lady of the house, too. She still felt a thrill of shock and desire whenever she thought about him coming into her bathroom like that. She doubted those sorts of things happened much among her conservative neighbors. But that kind of daring was one of the things she loved about Travis, one of the reasons she hadn't been able to get excited about a more conventional man.

Oh, Travis excited her, all right. When she turned the corner and saw his black truck parked in front of her house already, her skin flushed and her heart started beating faster. She hadn't expected him back so soon. She hoped he'd been so eager, he couldn't help but rush to her side.

He sat on the porch in her wicker rocker, holding Elizabeth on his lap and rocking slowly back and forth. He'd shoved his Stetson to the back of his head and unbuttoned his suede jacket. Even surrounded by white wicker and flowered cushions, he looked incredibly masculine, incredibly sexy. Elizabeth seemed drowsy, but she wasn't asleep.

"Sorry," Gwen called as she hurried toward the porch. "I took a little walk to work the kinks out. I didn't think you'd beat me home."

"You have kinks?" He watched her come toward him with that hot, penetrating look that melted her bones.

"Um, not really." She felt herself blushing. He must have thought she'd strained something during their morning lovemaking. "It was just an expression. I'm sorry I made you wait, though."

"No problem. We haven't been here long. But I think Lizzie's ready for her noontime bottle and a nap."

Gwen's pulse quickened. A nap for the baby could mean playtime for the adults. She had no doubt Travis was thinking exactly the same thing, especially after his comment about kinks. "What did Doc Harrison say about her cold?"

"We have it on the run." Travis smiled. "He was real pleased with how we got her through this. He says that he thinks her teething will be no sweat for us, now that we've weathered this cold."

"Teething?" Surprised, Gwen studied the baby. "So soon?"

"She'll be getting teeth before we know it, he said." A note of pride crept into his voice as he looked down at Elizabeth. "She's advanced for her age. She'll be an early crawler, he said."

Gwen was afraid he was setting himself up for heartbreak by making the assumption that Elizabeth would be around in a few weeks when she started teething, and later, when she started crawling. She hated to burst his bubble, but she thought someone should keep him rooted in reality.

"Jessica could show up between now and then," she reminded him gently.

Travis glanced up, and his eyes glinted with determination. "So what? She walked out on this kid."

"She probably had a good reason."

"She'd better hope to hell she did. Sebastian and I have talked about this, and unless she had a damned good reason, she's gonna have a legal fight on her hands if she expects to waltz back in and take this kid away. I have rights, too, assuming I'm Lizzie's father, which I'm sure I am."

"You'd want custody?" Hope blazed bright as she considered that Travis might be thinking of settling down.

The light went out of his eyes. "No, probably not."

"But you just said—"

"I'd want Sebastian and Matty to have her, though,

and they'd let me see her all I wanted. It would be almost like having her with me."

So he wasn't thinking of settling down. Glancing away while she battled her emotions, she took the key from her pocket and fit it into the lock. "Let's go in. I'll fix us some lunch while you give Elizabeth her bottle."

Travis stood and followed Gwen into the house. He'd hated seeing the disappointment on her face when he'd told her he wouldn't seek custody of Lizzie. The truth of the matter was that he'd love to have custody, but it wouldn't work. He couldn't be dragging the little girl to Utah for the winter and back to Colorado again for the summer. In Utah his mother could help with her, and would probably love it, but he wouldn't leave Lizzie there for the summer and be away from her all that time.

She needed a mother and a father, full-time, and that's what Sebastian and Matty could give her. They were ready and willing to do that, although part of Sebastian's urge came from his stubborn belief that *he* was Lizzie's father. Any fool could look at the baby and know that wasn't the case. She was Travis all over.

He was positive he'd crawled early, too. He'd done everything early, he thought with a grin as he remembered the incident with Cindy Rexford in the hayloft the summer he turned fifteen.

"Are we gonna have some of that soup?" he called out to Gwen as he took Lizzie upstairs to get rid of her outdoor clothes and his jacket.

"Not for lunch," Gwen called back. "It needs to simmer longer."

Travis paused on the stairs. "Leftover lasagna?"

"Sure."

As he continued up the stairs, he could almost taste that lasagna. Man, that woman could cook. And after lunch, when Lizzie had gone to sleep, then he and Gwen could snuggle up and...of course he was forgetting about the talk they needed to have. He would like to put that off, but he didn't think Gwen would let him do that.

He wished life could stay the way it was right now, with the three of them sharing this house and living so easily together. He didn't know about Gwen, but for him this was paradise. He had his baby near, the most delicious food he'd ever tasted, and a woman who satisfied him completely. What more could a man want? To have it go on forever, he thought with a sigh.

He brought Lizzie down for her bottle and discovered Gwen had it waiting on the table. "Thank you," he said. One more example of what it was like to have a woman like Gwen around, he thought. He sat down and fed Lizzie while he watched Gwen move around the kitchen getting lunch ready.

The room smelled like heaven with soup on the stove and lasagna warming in the oven. When he noticed the loaf of bread she was cutting didn't have any store wrapper on it, he realized she'd probably baked that, too.

"You're amazing," he said.

She paused in the act of slicing the bread and glanced at him. "Not really."

"Really. How many other women these days bake bread and do all this cooking?"

She resumed slicing the bread. "They don't because they've found better things to do. They run companies and discover medical cures or get elected to office. Or they run a ranch, like Matty. I'm outdated."

"Bull. And besides, you run a bed and breakfast. I'll bet a lot of people go broke trying that, but you seem to be doing great."

"Thanks for saying so."

He was surprised by how grateful she sounded, as if she didn't really think much of her contribution to the world. He thought her contribution was just about perfect. "You know, all those women who are company presidents and scientists and lawyers and God knows what else need a cozy place to rest and recover from all that stress. They need places like this and people like you."

She wrapped the bread in foil and popped it in the oven. "I hadn't thought of it like that."

"Well, think of it." He felt good, being able to say something that might make her see herself in a better light. She'd done that for him. He noticed that she had a little smile on her face as she set the table for lunch, and he liked to believe he'd helped put it there.

When he'd finished giving Lizzie her bottle, he made sure he got a good burp out of her. Then he stood. "She's really sleepy. I'll go change her and put her down before we eat."

Gwen's glance was almost shy. "Okay."

His body tightened with desire. The aroma of the lasagna made his mouth water, but he could always eat that later. Gwen was a hell of a lot more tempting right now. Maybe they wouldn't make it through lunch, after all.

He hurried upstairs and had Lizzie changed and down for her nap in record time. Before he went back downstairs he reached in the pocket of his jacket, took out the box he'd tucked in there and retrieved a couple of foil packets. The trip to Doc Harrison's had taken no time at all. He'd been able to swing by Sloan Drug on the way back to Gwen's house.

Gwen had the lasagna dished out by the time he walked into the kitchen, and she was putting the bread into a straw basket lined with flowered material. Everything she did had style, he thought. Even the smallest things. And especially the way she made love.

He looked at the lunch she'd gone to so much trouble to fix for them. Then he looked at her. He had no trouble making the choice, but the man he was trying to be would offer her one. "Gwen."

She glanced up from the bread basket.

"We could, um, keep lunch warm in the oven."

She gave him a long, serious look that didn't bode well for his chances. "We could, but we won't," she said. "While we eat, I want you to tell me what's keeping you from settling down with a wife and children."

He'd half expected her to ask him at the next opportunity, but he'd sure like to stall this discussion. "We could be wasting precious time talking. No telling how long Lizzie will sleep."

She walked over to the table, the breadbasket in her hand. "It's not a waste of time." Her gaze held his. "Our future depends on it."

His stomach lurched, and suddenly he wasn't hungry anymore. He gripped the back of the kitchen chair. "We don't have a future," he said. "That's what I've been trying to tell you. I'm a bad deal. We can enjoy a couple of days here, but then maybe we should just go our separate ways." His stomach hurt even more as he said that. He wasn't sure he could live through losing Gwen, but he couldn't think of any other option.

"You don't want that any more than I do. I can see it in your eyes."

"What I want and what I can have are two different things."

She slammed the breadbasket down on the table so hard the bread popped right out of it. "Dammit all, Travis, why is that?"

He swallowed. "Because I promised my dad before he died that I'd take care of my mother. For the rest of her life."

She stared at him as if he'd grown two heads, and then she started to smile. "That's all?" she said. "That's *it*?"

"That's enough." He might have figured she'd react this way. Most people would if they hadn't met Luann Evans. "You don't know my mother. She's high-maintenance. She—"

"Hold it right there." Gwen came around the table and cupped his face in both hands. "You are not going to put our happiness on hold because your mother needs you. No way." Her eyes glowed with purpose.

He'd never seen her look more beautiful. But she didn't understand a damned thing about this situation. "I can't leave her. I won't leave her. Not even for you, Gwen."

"I'm not asking you to do that," she murmured, edging up against him so he had no choice but to let go of the chair and grab her. "You can bring her here."

He laughed. "Oh, sure. Right. I'm sure that would work."

"Why wouldn't it? This is a big house. She could have her own room upstairs, unless she has trouble with stairs. In that case we could—"

"She doesn't have trouble with stairs." The velvet

outfit Gwen had on sure felt good when he wrapped his arms around her.

"So she's not handicapped, then. That's wonderful. I think she'd like the room in the back. It's bigger, and we might even be able to put in a small half-bath for her."

"You don't get it." He closed his eyes as she began moving sensuously against him, the velvet rubbing against the material of his shirt, the fullness of her breasts luring him. Much more of that and he wouldn't be able to think straight. "She wouldn't have trouble with the stairs, but she would have trouble with you," he said.

"Me? Why?"

His hands automatically cupped her behind and began a gentle kneading motion as he gazed into her eyes. Ah, she felt so good, looked so good, smelled so good.

"Why, Travis?"

He tried to remember what she'd asked him. Oh, yeah. Why his mother would have trouble with her. "Because she's used to being the boss in her house, and so are you."

"It's a big house." She ran her fingers through his hair. "We could work it out."

He loved her touch. Needed it. "And besides, she's used to having me all to herself. I'm the only kid. She's spoiled rotten, if you must know." He discovered her velvet pants had an elastic waist and he slipped his hands inside, encountering silk panties. His erection strained against his jeans. "But I promised my dad, and I'm keeping that promise."

"Of course you are." She cupped the back of his

head and urged him down toward her full, delicious mouth. "But you can do that here, with me."

"I don't think so." He could think of lots of things he'd like to do here with her, but co-existing with his mother wasn't on the list. Gwen was living in a dream world. But that didn't mean he didn't want to kiss her. That didn't mean he didn't want to make love to her until they were both wrung out and as limp as Lizzie's sock monkey.

"You're giving your mother too much power," she whispered, her breath soft against his mouth.

"You don't understand. She's—"

"Kiss me, Travis. And kiss me good."

He didn't need to be asked twice. With a groan he took the bounty she offered. She was so lush, so sweet, yet so bold. He wondered if kissing her would always remind him of that first time, when she'd used her mouth so generously to give him the most incredible pleasure of his life. He thrust his tongue deep, remembering.

He kissed her until they were both breathless and working at each other's clothes. He had the fastening on her bra undone and she'd pulled the snaps of his shirt open by the time they looked at each other and smiled.

"The lasagna's getting cold," she said.

"That's about the only thing that is." He slid his hands under her shirt and caressed her full breasts. "I'll bet your lasagna's good cold."

She pulled his shirt from the waistband of his jeans. "Want to find out?"

"Absolutely."

She ran her hands up his bare chest. "Travis, I want you to bring your mother here for a trial visit."

He shook his head. "You don't know what you're saying. It would be a disaster." He shivered as she leaned forward and kissed his nipples. "Do that again," he murmured.

"It wouldn't be a disaster." She ran her tongue over each tight nipple.

His breath caught. He liked that little maneuver. Liked it very much. There was so much they had yet to learn about each other. It would take a lifetime. "It would be a disaster," he said.

She stepped out of his arms, took both of his hands in hers, and began backing toward the door to her suite. "Come into my bedroom," she said softly, "and we can discuss it."

He gazed at her flushed face, her lips red from his kisses and her thick hair falling from its arrangement on top of her hair. He pictured taking that hair all the way down and burying his face in it. And that was just for starters. "Lady, I'd discuss inviting Godzilla for a trial visit if we can talk about it in your bedroom."

13

CLOTHES WERE A damn nuisance, Travis decided as he stood beside Gwen's four-poster struggling with her outfit while she helped him get rid of his. The only good part of the undressing was when he stopped to kiss whatever part of her body was currently available, but mostly he wanted to remove every stitch as quickly as possible so he could get down to business.

He used to be the king of the slow seduction, peeling a woman's clothes off inch by tantalizing inch, teasing her with the long unveiling. It seemed like a stupid game he didn't have time for now. This was for real.

While he pulled off his last sock, Gwen turned and threw back the comforter on the bed, filling the room with the delicate scent of lavender. Then she climbed in. He followed, and promptly sank into what felt like a giant marshmallow.

"What the heck?" Without quite meaning to, he rolled on top of her and nearly lost her in the billowy mattress.

She laughed as she wrapped her arms around him. "Feather bed. Extra thick, extra soft."

"No kidding. Put another one of these things on top of us and we could be shipped anywhere without getting broken." When he tried to lever himself up on his outstretched arms, his hands sank in past his wrists.

"A guy could have trouble getting any traction on this thing," he warned, waggling his eyebrows at her.

She smiled up at him. "I'm confident you'll find a way."

"Guess I'll have to keep myself steady as best I can." He leaned down and nuzzled her breasts. "Ah. Here's an outcropping I can latch on to for balance." He captured a nipple in his mouth and drew it in.

She sighed and arched upward. "That works."

Oh, it sure did. He began to get the hang of maneuvering in the fluffy mattress, and they were definitely *in* it and not *on* it. As he felt more cradled and less smothered, he began thinking he could get used to making love this way. As long as he had Gwen, he'd learn to make love standing on his head, if that was the only available option.

Her bedroom was dappled with sun filtered through the lace curtains over her windows, and he made the most of this daylight chance to love her with his eyes as well as his touch. Her skin was golden and smooth, and he had to pay close attention, deliciously close attention, before he found the small birthmark on her left breast, over her heart. The freckle on the inside of her right thigh took even more effort to locate, but once he found it, he decided to linger and explore the territory thoroughly.

She writhed beneath him, bringing his need to a frenzied pitch with her eagerness. "Please," she cried, breathing hard. "Now, Travis."

"Hope I can make it back into position," he said as the mattress billowed with his movements. "Roadblocks," he said, managing a grin even though his heart was pumping a mile a minute. "Always...road..." His grin faded as he absorbed the sweet invitation of her body beneath his and the glow in her eyes as she shifted, opening her thighs. His body quivered in anticipation when he realized how easily he could slip right into her, how easy it would be to forget birth control and love this woman the way she should be loved.

Damn, he was crazy about her. The idea of making her pregnant with his child kept swirling through his mind. He was pretty sure he'd accidentally fathered Lizzie, and now he understood how sad that was, when the most complete joy he could imagine would be creating a child on purpose with a woman he loved. *The* woman he loved. This woman.

He managed to reach the condom on the bedside table. "I want you like you wouldn't believe," he said, panting. "But you'll have to help. If I try to balance on this mattress while I put this thing on, I'm liable to kill us both."

She took the package immediately, tore it open and tossed the wrapping away. Then she did the most arousing thing he'd ever experienced. Holding his gaze through the entire process, she reached down and carefully, expertly sheathed him without once losing eye contact. She did the whole thing by feel. By the time she'd finished, he was a lit fuse.

"Now," she murmured, lifting her hips as she continued to look into his eyes.

"Yes, now." He pushed home, glorying in her soft cry of pleasure and the way her face seemed lit from within. This was good. So good.

He marveled at how easy it was to make love when you were holding the right woman. No thought of technique. Only the wonder of sinking deep, followed by the warm friction of retreat, all the while anticipat-

ing the fun waiting for him on the next forward thrust.
He and Gwen moved with such togetherness that he
didn't know if he matched her beat or she matched
his. Or if they'd created this special rhythm together.

All he knew was that he'd found something rare,
something he would never find again with any other
woman. She urged him on, faster, faster, faster. He
watched her eyes widen and her breathing grow ragged. Her gaze burned into his as she dug her fingers
into his hips.

"Kiss me now," she said, gasping. "So I don't wake
the baby."

His heart bursting with love for her, he leaned
down and took her cries of release into his mouth, and
then he let her absorb his. His body rocked with the
force of his climax, jolted as if he'd been hit by lightning, and he kissed her so hard he felt the imprint of
her teeth against his mouth.

When their cries softened to whimpers, he lifted his
mouth from hers and kissed her gently. Then he sank
against her soft breasts while his body continued to
celebrate with little rocket bursts of sensation.

She stroked his hair and took a shaky breath. "End
of discussion," she murmured.

"Discussion?" He could barely move, let alone
think.

"Can you live without this?"

The answer came before he could censor it. "No."

"Neither can I." She took another shaky breath. "So
you have to bring your mother here. We have to try
it."

He supposed they did. The joy he'd experienced
here in this bed with Gwen was a miracle. He closed

his eyes and prayed there were more where that came from. "Okay. We'll try it."

SEVERAL DAYS LATER Gwen's stomach churned with nervousness as she gazed across the kitchen table at Matty. "Good Lord, what have I done?"

"The right thing," Matty assured her, reaching over to squeeze her hand. She'd packed up Elizabeth and driven into town to spend the afternoon with Gwen while she waited for Travis and his mother to arrive. Mother and son had left Utah the day before and had spent the night in Durango. They were due any minute.

Gwen desperately needed the moral support Matty was providing, even though the plan had been entirely her idea. But she'd discovered that once Travis had committed to it, he was hell-bent to see it through. He said they had to find out if it was a workable plan, or if, as he predicted, it was the worst idea of the new millennium.

He'd reminded her that Matty and Sebastian would begin running cattle soon and he'd be needed for that, so if they were going to entertain his mother, it had to be right away. The minute Matty and Sebastian had returned from their honeymoon, Travis had driven to Utah to invite his mother to spend a week at Hawthorne House. Gwen didn't know what he'd said to convince her, but she'd agreed.

And Gwen had the horrible feeling she'd bitten off more than she could chew. "Maybe I should have held off for a few months, until fall."

Matty put down her coffee cup. "Why? Strike while the iron is hot, I say."

"Ga-ga!" shouted Elizabeth from her position on Matty's lap.

Matty smiled down at the baby. "See? Even Elizabeth agrees with me." She glanced back across the table at Gwen. "You have to try to make this work with Travis, and there's no time like the present to get started." She grinned. "Speaking from experience, the honeymoon alone is worth all the aggravation these guys put us through."

"I'm happy you had a great time." Gwen was also glad she and Travis hadn't called them when the baby got sick, for many reasons. Sure as the world, Matty and Sebastian would have cut short their honeymoon, and Travis and Gwen would never have discovered each other.

"Great doesn't even begin to describe it," Matty said. "Except for the one day we checked out private detectives, we did nothing but play."

"You both needed that. You work so hard." She took a drink of her coffee and decided she should make a new pot, so it would be fresh when Luann Evans arrived. She stood. "Excuse me. I'm going to make coffee."

"This is only ten minutes old, Gwen."

"I'm making fresh coffee." She ignored Matty's sigh and walked over to the counter. "You know I have mixed emotions about putting a detective on Jessica's trail." She ground the beans swiftly and poured them into the coffee filter. "In a way, considering she might have conceived Elizabeth with Travis, I'd rather not drag her back here and have to deal with her. I know that's selfish, but—"

"If it is, then I'm guilty of the same thing. Don't forget it might have been Sebastian she slept with."

"Do you really think so?" Gwen couldn't imagine Sebastian in that role at all.

"I think it's possible. I found out he gets pretty wild and crazy when he's had a few drinks. I'd never seen that side of him, but in Denver the hotel gave us a bottle of champagne, which we polished off, and Sebastian really...well, um..."

Gwen turned to stare at her friend. "Matty! You're blushing!" She loved it. If she'd ever been worried that Sebastian was too tame for Matty, she could forget that concern right now. She added the water to the pot and started it perking before she returned to the table and sat down. "Are you going to tell me about it?"

"Nope." Matty fanned her red face with her hand. "Let's just say that I think it's entirely possible that this baby belongs to Sebastian."

"My goodness." Gwen couldn't stop grinning. "Still waters run deep, I guess. Okay, so we don't know whose kid she is, at this point."

"No, and that's just it. I think we have to get it settled. We can't have those two guys wrangling over this baby forever. It might work as a TV sitcom, but in real life, it sucks." Matty took another sip of her coffee. "Which reminds me, how are you planning to explain Elizabeth to Travis's mother?"

That problem sobered Gwen up real quick. "I've thought about that."

"I can imagine."

"Travis and I considered having him tell her about the baby on the way over, but then we were afraid that would put her in a bad mood before she ever got here. I mean, how can she be happy about Elizabeth? Either the baby's proof that her son got drunk and acted irresponsibly, or Elizabeth's not even her granddaughter. But that's the only way to present it to her. We're not going to lie, because if Elizabeth is Travis's baby, then Luann will be a part of her life."

"True." Matty gave Elizabeth a spoon to play with and the little girl banged it on Matty's arm. "I sure hope Luann is flexible."

"Travis gave me the impression she's very *in*flexible." Gwen's stomach began to knot. She watched Elizabeth sucking on the spoon and pushed back her chair. "I think I'll polish the silver."

"Gwen, sit down. The silver doesn't need polishing."

"Maybe not. But you know what? I think I forgot to dust the windowsills." She started to get up again.

"For heaven's sake, sit down. Do you want your future mother-in-law to find you with a feather duster in your hand? That sets a terrible precedent, if you ask me. Might as well put on an apron and a little cap to go with it, because you'll be cast in the role of maid for the rest of your association with her."

Gwen sighed and leaned her head in her hands. "Maybe she's not as bad as Travis makes her out to be."

"I'm sure she's not."

Gwen lifted her head to look at Matty. "But after the way he's talked, I can't help picturing some six-foot-tall, overbearing, demanding, obnoxious bully of a woman."

"She's six feet tall?"

"Well, Travis never exactly said, but—"

"Anybody home?" called a deep male voice.

Gwen's heart lurched into a faster rhythm and her

mouth went dry. She clutched her coffee cup in both hands and stared at Matty. "Oh, God. They're here."

"Hang tough," Matty murmured. "You're the best thing that ever happened to her son, and don't you forget it."

An unfamiliar female voice floated in from the porch. "These wild colors on the outside make it look like a cathouse, son."

Gwen glanced at Matty.

Matty raised her eyebrows and squared her shoulders. "It does *not*," she said under her breath to Gwen.

"I like it, Mom," Travis said, his voice getting closer. "It's cheerful. Hey, Gwen, where are you?"

He'd risen to her defense. Gwen loved him more at that moment than she ever had before. "Coming!" she called. She gave Matty a shaky smile and stood, smoothing her hair and straightening the skirt of her dress. "Do I look like a Madam?" she asked Matty.

"Of course not!"

"Then here goes nothing." Heart pounding, she walked into the hall.

She nearly collided with Travis.

"Hey, there." He caught her by the shoulders and gave her one quick glance of approval. "Nice." But he didn't kiss her, Gwen noticed. He turned. "Mom, I'd like you to meet Gwen Hawthorne. Gwen, this is my mother, Luann Evans."

The hallway was cool, but Gwen felt sweat trickle down her back. She widened her mouth in what she hoped was a smile and not a grimace as she braced herself for the Amazon woman she expected to be filling the hallway with her bulk.

But Luann Evans was *tiny*. The front door stood open, blocked by a large suitcase, and the light coming from it cast her in shadow, but she couldn't be more than five feet tall, and probably wore a size two dress. Her suitcase was bigger than she was.

Gwen controlled the desire to laugh. Travis jumped through hoops for this little bitty thing? She stepped forward and her eyes adjusted to the dim light of the hall.

Luann wore her gray hair cropped short and obviously didn't believe in hair dye or makeup to disguise her fifty-something years. She wore jeans and a sweatshirt, and her eyes were the same tawny gold as Travis's.

Gwen decided this would be a piece of cake. She stretched out her hand. "Mrs. Evans, it's a pleasure."

Luann grasped her hand, and her grip was extremely firm. Amazingly firm and strong, for such a small woman. "Call me Luann."

"All right." Gwen smiled. Yes, this would be just fine. Travis had exaggerated the problem.

Luann released Gwen's hand. "And we might as well get this out in the open right now. Are you sleeping with my son?"

Gwen's mouth dropped open. She glanced at Travis, who had suddenly bolted toward the door, abandoning her.

"Let me get this suitcase upstairs for you, Mom," he said. "Would you like to freshen up? Your bathroom's upstairs, right next to your bedroom, and I'm sure you'll love it. The wallpaper's curling a bit, but that will be fixed soon. Gwen has those cute little soaps you like, the ones with the pictures that stay in the soap clear through."

"Never mind about my bedroom and little soaps and wallpaper, son." Luann didn't take her gaze from

Gwen's. "I'm more concerned with your sleeping arrangements at the moment."

Gwen felt heat climbing into her cheeks. She waited to see if Travis would step forward and say something, but he lingered by the suitcase, as if ready to take his cue from her.

Apparently he hadn't made his relationship with her crystal clear to his mother. But she could hardly blame him. The idea was to win Luann over, not throw their sexuality in her face. Still, she'd vowed to be honest with this woman from the first, so now was not the time to tell a lie, even a socially acceptable, little white one.

She cleared her throat and gathered her courage. "Yes, Luann, I am sleeping with your son."

Luann nodded.

Gwen let out her breath in grateful relief. The woman had accepted the situation gracefully. One hurdle crossed.

"I'd like you to stop doing that," Luann said.

"What?" This time Gwen heard Travis echo her question.

He came forward. "Listen, Mom, I don't think that's any of your—"

"I'm a guest in your home, Gwen," Luann said, still looking directly at her. "This is an old house. I don't want to have to put up with any thumping and bumping in the night. It's unseemly for a mother to hear those kinds of goings-on."

Score one for Luann, Gwen thought. She *was* a guest, and no telling how much sound carried from downstairs. Now that Gwen thought about it, she remembered being privy to a few thumps and bumps coming from upstairs over the years of running the bed and breakfast. Couples came for a getaway, after all.

Of course she and Travis would have been very careful. In fact, they might have been so intimidated they might have stayed celibate the entire week, although Gwen wasn't sure they could have stood that. But what could she do, assure Luann that she and Travis would be quiet when they made love?

"Uh, you have a point, Luann," Gwen said. "I'm sure Travis will be happy to sleep upstairs in the bedroom next to yours during the week of your visit."

Travis definitely *didn't* look happy. His scowl could have curdled milk. Gwen glanced at him with a small smile. She was inventive. They'd loan his mother one of their trucks and suggest she explore the town. Or Gwen would bribe Matty to invite Luann to the ranch for lunch. They'd get her out of the house one way or another, at least for a couple of hours.

But if all went well and Luann agreed to move here and live with them, Gwen would have the downstairs suite soundproofed. There was no way she'd spend years sneaking around to make love to Travis.

Luann looked as pleased as Travis looked displeased. "Thank you for honoring an old lady's wishes," she said with a queenly nod of her head.

From the kitchen doorway came the distinctive sound of someone blowing a raspberry. Gwen turned to find Matty standing there holding Elizabeth. Gwen had been so absorbed in dealing with Luann that she'd completely forgotten Matty and Elizabeth were in the kitchen.

Elizabeth looked at them, stuck her little tongue out and blew again, spraying spit everywhere.

"My thoughts, exactly," Travis muttered.

Luann brightened. "What a darling baby!" She glanced at Matty. "Are you her mother?"

"Uh, no," Gwen cut in. "Luann, this is my friend Matty Lang. Matty, this is Travis's mother."

"Nice to meet you," Matty said without much inflection.

Gwen could tell Matty was still ticked about the cathouse remark. Plus she'd probably overheard the whole song and dance about who was sleeping where and had decided she wasn't a fan of Travis's mother. But Gwen wasn't ready to make a negative judgment yet. After all, her own mother wasn't a very warm and fuzzy person, either. Plus her mother was never around these days.

And at least Luann liked babies. She was gazing adoringly at Elizabeth, as if she could hardly wait to get her hands on the little munchkin.

"So," Luann said, clasping her hands in front of her, "who does this sweet child belong to, may I ask?"

Gwen decided she'd handled the first bombshell, and Travis could handle this one. She gave him a pointed look.

He shifted his weight and adjusted the tilt of his Stetson. "Actually, Mom, there's a good chance this baby's mine."

14

TRAVIS HAD NEVER THOUGHT much about the concept of heaven and hell before, but now he knew exactly what each was like. Heaven was like the time he'd spent with Gwen after Lizzie had recovered from her cold. But the past four days with his mother in the house had definitely been hell.

She'd decided that he was some sort of sex fiend who'd impregnated one woman and now was cavorting mindlessly with another one. Except there would be no cavorting on his mother's watch. Nosiree. She refused to let him out of her sight, and she was constantly finding things for him to do for her, like hauling her to the store for this or that, and driving her around to see the sights. She wouldn't take the truck herself and do that, oh, no. She wanted Travis.

And Gwen kept encouraging him to humor his mother. They wanted his mother to like Colorado, Gwen said, so the more he showed her a good time, the more likely she'd agree to move here. Maybe so, but he doubted it, and he was so desperate to make love to Gwen that he was considering luring her out in the backyard some night, chilly and uncomfortable though that would be.

He wasn't even sure Gwen would agree to a plan like that. She seemed to think they shouldn't try to trick his mother, either, and that they should honor their promise to her not to fool around while she was in the house. Gwen seemed to think that if they demonstrated their consideration, his mother would eventually thaw and give them both her blessing. In a pig's eye.

The only bright spot was that Luann seemed to have fallen hard for Lizzie. Travis wasn't surprised his mother loved the baby. Everyone did. Funny, though, how his mother could lecture him for hours about his unforgivable mistake in getting Jessica pregnant and still go all gaga when Matty brought Lizzie around for a visit.

Gwen had put great store by that, and on the fact that Luann seemed interested in all Gwen's domestic projects. Today Gwen was giving Luann a weaving lesson and he'd felt in the way, so he'd driven out to help Sebastian repair a section of fence before the cattle arrived the following week.

It felt good to saddle up and ride out with Sebastian, and if this thing with his mother hadn't been driving him nuts, he'd be looking forward to the summer. He'd be looking forward to his whole damn life, come to think of it.

"I can hardly wait until Elizabeth's old enough to ride," Sebastian said as they trotted their horses along the fence line of the south pasture.

"Me, either. Once she can sit up by herself, I thought I'd put her on in front of me and take her for a little walk, just around the corral." Travis liked that mental picture of Lizzie and him tucked into the saddle, cruising around on a warm summer day, with Gwen looking on, so proud. He sighed. There was only one dang fly in the ointment. His mother.

Sebastian glanced over at him. "From that frown on

your puss I take it you're thinking about the situation with your mother."

"Yep."

"Gwen's gonna get her to come around. Don't give up yet."

Travis shook is head. "I've known my mother longer than any of you. There's no way she'll move into another woman's house and play second fiddle for the rest of her life. No way. Gwen's catering to her now, making her feel like she's in charge of our lives, but that couldn't go on if she was really living with us. Nope, in the end she'll refuse to cooperate. I can feel it coming."

"I think you underestimate Gwen. I—" Sebastian paused as his cell phone buzzed.

Travis jumped. "Every time I hear that damn thing I think it's a rattler."

"I know." Travis reached back and took the phone out of his saddlebag. "But I can't leave Matty with no way to contact me. Not with the baby to think of. And Jessica." He punched a button on the phone. "Hello?"

Travis kicked his big bay into a canter, to give Sebastian some privacy for his conversation. Probably just lovey-dovey talk between Sebastian and Matty. The two of them couldn't stand being apart, but they couldn't take the baby out on every ranch chore. This time Matty had stayed behind.

But seconds later Sebastian called out to Travis. "How'd you like to spend some quality time with Gwen?"

Travis pulled the gelding to a skidding stop and turned in the saddle. "You mean *quality* time?"

Sebastian winked. "That's what I'm talking about, cowboy."

"But how? My mother—"

"Matty's taken pity on you and come up with a plan," Sebastian said as he drew alongside Travis and reined in his horse. "Are you up for that?"

Travis laughed. "I am so up for that."

"I thought so." Sebastian put the phone back to his ear. "It's a go. Yeah. I'm sure he'll be forever grateful. Love you, too. Bye." He pushed the disconnect button and put the phone back in his saddlebag.

"How's she going to work this?" Travis asked.

"She'll call Hawthorne House and beg for Gwen and Luann's help. She'll say she needs Gwen to follow her into Hennessy's Garage because she has to drop off her truck to be worked on, and then she needs to do some yarn shopping and desperately wants Gwen's advice. She'd take the baby, except that Elizabeth has been fussing lately, probably because a tooth is about to come through. She'll ask Luann to babysit."

Travis stared at Sebastian. "But she doesn't really want Gwen to follow her to the garage or help pick out yarn, right?"

Sebastian grinned. "I knew you were smarter than you looked."

Travis tried not to let his eagerness show, but it was no use. "Hot damn. How long before I should head back to the house?"

Sebastian clucked to his horse and set off down the fence line. "Matty says give her an hour to set everything in motion. If she runs into any snags, she'll call us, but she's seen the way Luann looks at that baby. The woman is dying to have that kid to herself. She'll probably be so happy about that prospect that she won't smell a rat."

Travis kept his gelding even with Sebastian's. "Is Matty going to tell Gwen the plan? Because Gwen has been insisting we have to play this straight, you know. She doesn't want to chance getting my mother riled up."

"Yeah, and Matty thinks Gwen might have some moral objection at first, which Matty thinks is silly. So she's not saying a word until they get to the garage and Luann's already settled in with the baby at the ranch house. Then Matty's gonna tell Gwen to hightail it home because there's a hot cowboy waiting for her. At that point she thinks Gwen will go along with the program."

Travis couldn't stop smiling. "Did I ever tell you that you're married to a very terrific lady?"

"Once or twice. Now shake a leg. We need to mend as much fence as we can before you leave. All this romance is playing hell with the ranching business."

GWEN THOUGHT it was a little strange that Matty had picked this particular day to get her truck fixed. It had been shifting poorly every since she'd nearly stripped the gears back when she was spaced out on wedding plans, but she'd never indicated that fixing the truck was a top priority, especially considering that she could use Sebastian's Bronco whenever she needed a vehicle. Still, Gwen wasn't about to deny a friend a favor, and Luann had been overjoyed at the prospect of baby-sitting for Elizabeth.

So Gwen dutifully followed Matty to Hennessy's Garage and sat in her purple truck waiting for Matty to come out of the small office attached to the double-bay garage. She rolled the window down and breathed in the flower-scented air. Spring had arrived in Huerfano, and even Hennessy's had a little window box of daffodils blooming merrily away.

Eventually Matty came out, but instead of climbing in the truck with Gwen, she walked around to the driver's side.

"Is something wrong?" Gwen asked.

Matty smiled and tucked her thumbs in the pockets of her jeans. "Nope. I just came to tell you that I won't need your help after all. Jake Hennessy's going to loan me his Jeep to do my errands, so you're welcome to go home if you like."

Gwen felt a flash of irritation. This was so unlike Matty, roping her into something unnecessary, especially when her life was so complicated already these days. "What about Luann? Shouldn't I go to the ranch and help her with Elizabeth?"

Matty gazed at her, that same little smile on her face. "No, I think you should go home and spend some time with Travis."

Gwen's irritation rose to the surface. "Travis isn't there! As you well know. He's out riding fence with Sebastian." Gwen hesitated as Matty continued to give her that knowing look. "Isn't he?"

Matty slowly shook her head. "He's at Hawthorne House, waiting for you."

Gwen gasped as she finally understood what was going on. "You set this whole thing up, didn't you?"

"Somebody had to beat Luann Evans at her own game, and it sure didn't look like you had the heart for it. Now you don't have to follow through, of course. If it bothers your conscience too much, I'll tell Jake I don't need the loan of his vehicle, after all. But if you can see your way clear to cooperate, I figure you and Travis have about two hours to kill."

Excitement built quickly, and her voice quivered when she spoke. "But when I took Luann out to your place, I saw Travis's truck parked over by the barn."

Matty nodded. "And a little more than two hours from now, it'll be parked there again. Don't worry. Luann's not going to leave that baby to go prowling around the barn checking on whether Travis's truck is still there."

Gwen began to smile. "No, I guess she won't."

"Go on, now. You're wasting time."

Gwen reached for the ignition key, her hand shaking from anticipation. "Matty, I already feel guilty about fooling Travis's mother like this."

"A little guilt adds some spice to the experience, don't you think?"

Gwen looked at her friend and laughed. "Guess I'm about to find out."

"Have fun."

Gwen lifted her hand in farewell and pulled out into the street. She had to force herself to drive the speed limit through the little town as she pictured Travis waiting for her. She'd caught the looks of frustration he'd thrown her way in the past few days. A man like Travis didn't take well to frustration.

For that matter, Gwen hadn't weathered the dry spell very well, either. She'd slept poorly and had increasingly erotic dreams whenever she did manage to fall asleep. But thanks to Matty's devious plans, she would feel Travis's arms around her again, experience the sweet urgency of his mouth, the driving force of his... Gwen slammed on her brakes. She'd nearly missed a stop sign.

She concentrated on the road after that, but when she turned down her street and saw Travis's black truck in front of Hawthorne House, her hands began to shake. She'd never been such a basket case over a man, and the intensity of her emotions frightened her a little. If Luann refused to consider moving to Colorado... Gwen shoved the thought aside. Luann would agree to move. She had to. Gwen couldn't imagine life without Travis.

She parked behind Travis's truck and hurried up the walk. The minute she started up the steps, the front door opened. He'd been watching for her.

He stood back from the door, holding it open for her. He'd never looked sexier. His voice rumbled low in his chest. "Get in here, woman."

Heart pounding, she crossed the porch and stepped through the door.

He grabbed her, kicking the door shut with his foot as he pushed her up against the wall. She'd never in her wildest dreams imagined being flattened against this flower-sprigged wallpaper and kissed until she couldn't breathe. When Travis began taking off her slacks, she figured out that more than kissing would happen in this hallway, barely inside her front door.

Desire flooded through her, drenching her completely. She fumbled with his belt, unfastening it as he wrenched her zipper down and shoved his hand inside her panties. Without hesitation he pushed his fingers inside her, as if he expected to find her exactly as she was, hot and wet. She gripped the waistband of his jeans and whimpered with pleasure.

He lifted his mouth a fraction from hers, and he was panting. "Finish your job. Condom's in my left shirt pocket." He pressed the heel of his hand against her damp curls.

"Oh, my. *Travis.*"

"I thought you'd never get here." His mouth came down on hers again as he stroked her with one hand and used the other to shove down her slacks and panties. She arched against the movement of his fingers, but she managed to unzip his jeans. Jeans and belt hit the hardwood floor with a clunk as she pulled down his briefs, freeing his erection.

"Hurry," he mumbled against her lips. *"Please, hurry."*

He was making her so crazy she couldn't remember which was his left shirt pocket and she groped around in the wrong one for the condom. When he growled low in his throat, she switched pockets and found the condom. It seemed to take forever, but at last she had it on.

He drew back slightly, and his breath was hot on her mouth. "Brace...your hands on my...shoulders," he said, gasping.

She gripped his shoulders. He cupped her bottom and lifted her up against the wall. Her slacks and panties slipped down her legs to the floor just before he thrust into her with a soft cry of triumph.

His fullness inside her brought tears of happiness to her eyes. She had missed him so much. She wrapped her legs around his hips in welcome.

She held on, her back flat against the wall as he gripped her bottom and surged into her with enough force to shake the wall. A picture hanging on the parlor side clattered to the floor. Travis didn't even pause.

Nor did she want him to. The pressure built to an exquisite pitch, and then, with one swift upward thrust, he set her free. Laughing with joy, tears streaming down her face, she came apart. With a guttural sound of satisfaction, he followed her, his body shuddering against hers as he held her tight against the wall and leaned his forehead against hers.

Gradually his breathing slowed, but he still held her firmly, still stayed deep inside her as he lifted his head to look into her eyes. "I love you," he said quietly.

Fresh tears filled her eyes. "You've never said."

"Ah, but you had to know."

She nodded. "I knew. But I still needed to hear it."

"Sorry it took so long." He gave her a crooked smile. "I wouldn't mind hearing it from you, either."

"Oh, Travis, of course I love you." She'd told him so many times in her imagination that it came as a shock that she'd never said the words out loud.

His gaze heated. "That sure sounds good, especially considering the week we're having." He kissed her tenderly, then drew back with a sigh. "I don't think my mother will agree to move here."

She didn't want this moment to be spoiled by gloom and doom. "Don't give up yet."

"Okay, but even if she doesn't, I will." He looked into her eyes. "I will, Gwen. I want you to marry me."

Her throat tightened as she realized the sacrifice he was willing to make, the guilt he was willing to endure, for her. "Of course I want that, too, but I can't ask you to go back on your promise," she said softly.

"You didn't ask. I'm telling you what I'm prepared to do."

"But—"

He silenced her with a kiss, a kiss that soon became sensual and suggestive. His lips slid down to her throat. "Let's not talk about it now," he murmured against her skin. "We have some catching up to do."

Her pulse quickened. "I thought...we just did."

His tongue dipped into the hollow of her throat and

he chuckled. "Oh, sweetheart, that was only to take the edge off. Now we can get down to some serious loving."

Although she'd felt thoroughly loved a moment ago, Gwen felt the passion rise in her again. "Which room would you like to try next?"

He eased her to her feet. "I had the parlor in mind. That fainting couch has possibilities. Oh, and Gwen?"

"Yes?"

"I'm moving back to your bedroom tonight."

GWEN TRIED to talk him out of moving into her bedroom. She thought they had a better chance of winning Luann over if they went along with her wishes and didn't openly sleep together during this trial visit. But making love to her after four days of celibacy seemed to have flipped a switch in Travis. He was no longer interested in compromise.

He made no effort to hide the fact he was moving back to Gwen's room, and every night he reached for her, as if to prove he could make love to her whether his mother approved or not. Gwen couldn't resist him, even when she suspected his reasons weren't entirely pure. Still, although it wasn't easy to do, she kept their lovemaking extremely quiet.

Luann couldn't have been bothered by any noise from their bedroom activities, Gwen knew, yet Travis's mother seemed to have picked up the gauntlet he'd thrown down. In the last days of her stay her jaw seemed to tighten with a secret resolution. Gwen was afraid she'd resolved not to give Travis and Gwen her blessing, let alone agree to live with them in Colorado.

Gwen watched the widening rift between mother

and son with anxiety. She couldn't imagine Travis would be happy if he became estranged from his mother, despite his big talk, and Luann would be downright miserable. She apparently had nobody besides Travis.

Gwen found herself compensating by urging Luann to relax instead of helping around the house, as she'd done the first four days of the week. Gwen even let some of her own chores go and took Luann into Canon City for lunch one day, and out to Matty's for lunch and a chance to play with Elizabeth another day.

Her efforts didn't do much to loosen the set of Luann's jaw.

Travis probably knew they were headed for disaster, but he wouldn't discuss it with Gwen during any of the private times they had together. So they stumbled through until Luann's last night at Hawthorne House. Travis had decided that during dinner they'd announce their plans to marry and ask Luann if she'd be willing to move permanently to Colorado.

Gwen worked most of the day on the meal, and because she wanted Luann to feel special, she'd politely refused her offer of help. Instead she'd suggested Travis take her on a day trip to the Royal Gorge. They both returned from the outing in such a sour mood that Gwen wondered if she'd done the right thing sending them off together.

While they both went to wash up, she put the finishing touches on the table, lit the candles and adjusted the bouquet of flowers she'd bought for the centerpiece. She knew the beef was tender, the vegetables steamed perfectly, the salad crisp, the dressing imaginative, but she'd never been so nervous about the outcome of a meal in her life.

Travis and his mother arrived at the table at the same time.

"Smells great," Travis said. He walked over to Gwen, pulled her close and kissed her full on the mouth. "I missed you."

Gwen blushed and drew back from his embrace, a question in her eyes. Despite his defiant move back to Gwen's bedroom, he'd never been so blatantly affectionate with Gwen in front of his mother. "I missed you, too," she said.

"Don't mind me," Luann said, pulling out a chair. "I can dish myself. Unless you need this table for something else. In which case I'll just take my plate to my room. No problem."

Gwen extricated herself from Travis's arms. "Luann, we didn't mean to offend you. We—"

"Love each other," Travis finished for her. "We love each other, Mom, and we're going to get married. Soon."

Luann gazed at him, and her eyes grew bright. "It's no more than I expected. Been acting like a couple of rabbits."

Gwen opened her mouth to protest, but she noticed that the brightness in Luann's eyes came from a delicate sheen of tears. The woman was about to cry. Oh, dear. "We want you to come and live with us," she said quickly.

Luann pushed back her chair and stood. "I'd sooner hang by my teeth from the Royal Gorge Bridge." Then she left the room.

Gwen started to go after her. "Luann, please don't—"

Travis caught her arm. "Let her go," he said in a tense, angry voice. "I *knew* she'd be like this!"

Gwen turned to look at him. "You set her up to be like this, by kissing me right in front of her."

"There is no reason I shouldn't!"

"Maybe not eventually, but right here in the beginning, it looked to me like you were goading her. And it sure worked. I'm going up there to try and straighten things out."

His grip tightened on her arm. "Don't you dare go up there and beg her."

Gwen gazed at him. "Why not? Why not beg her to reconsider? What have we got to lose?"

"Our pride!"

"To hell with our pride!" She shook her arm from his grasp. "I'm going to talk to her."

"It won't do any good, I tell you!" His eyes blazed with anger. "She's going to cut off her nose to spite her face. If she can't have me all to herself, then she doesn't want me at all. I knew she'd be that way, and by God, she didn't disappoint me. Well, I'm finished with her. She's run my life long enough!"

Gwen was surprised at the force of his anger. "I can't see the harm in trying to reason with her. Maybe she just needs time to think about this. I think we should leave the door open, so that she can—"

"Don't you understand? This is the *first thing* I've ever asked her to do for me. The *first thing*. And she can't even consider it. What kind of mother would be that way?"

Slowly Gwen began to understand. Travis had learned a few lessons in parenting recently thanks to Elizabeth, and he was freshly acquainted with the fact that parenting involved sacrifice. It had been gnawing at him that his mother didn't seem the type to sacrifice for him. Once upon a time he might have thought she loved him too much. Now he was afraid she didn't love him at all.

But Gwen didn't believe that for a minute. She'd seen the look on Luann's face each time Travis walked into a room. "Let me talk to her, Travis. I think we just don't appreciate how hard this must be for her, but I—"

"Don't even think about trying to sweet-talk her into staying. Not now. Not with that reaction. I don't want her here."

Gwen was losing patience with his stubbornness. "You can't mean that."

"I mean it! Damn it, I mean exactly that! And I'm sick to death of debating it with you. I'm going for a drive." He left the room. Moments later she heard the front door slam and then his truck roared to life.

Gwen gazed at the flickering candles and the little vase of roses in the middle of the table. The scene she'd worked so hard to create began to blur as tears dripped silently down her cheeks.

15

BY THE TIME Travis pulled up in front of the log-style ranch house at the Rocking D he'd cooled down some, but he was still furious with his mother. He used to take it for granted that he had to organize his life around her, because that's what his father had taught him to do.

But he'd watched Matty and Sebastian rearrange their whole lives for Lizzie. Hell, he'd rearranged his whole life, too. Without asking, he knew Gwen was prepared to do the same for Lizzie or other children they might have. It was what parents did.

In the past week he'd come to realize that his mother had no right to control his life the way she'd been doing. He'd still look out for her as he'd promised, but on his own terms. If she wouldn't move to Colorado, then he'd hire somebody to help her get through the long Utah winter. She wouldn't like that, but he didn't much care. She'd had things her way long enough.

He crossed the wide front porch and rapped on the front door of the ranch house. He had a strong need to see his baby girl.

Sebastian came to the door chewing a mouthful of food. He swallowed. "Hey, Travis. Where's the rest of the gang?"

"Still in town. Sorry. I guess I interrupted your dinner."

"No problem." Sebastian looked curious as hell but he didn't ask any questions. "We just got a call I'm sure you'll be interested in hearing about. Come on in."

Travis stepped into the rustic living room with its huge rock fireplace and comfortable furniture. He took off his Stetson. "Jessica?"

"No, but it has to do with her. Hey, Matty," he called as he headed for the dining room. "Look who's here."

Matty sat in a dining chair making an attempt to eat while she gave Lizzie a bottle. "What a coincidence. Hi, Travis. We were just talking about you."

"Yeah, Sebastian said something about a phone call." Travis took a seat next to Matty and hung his hat on the back of his chair. "Why don't you let me give her the rest of that bottle so you can finish your dinner?"

"I'll accept that offer." Matty eased the bottle away from Lizzie and set it on the table before lifting the baby and transferring her to Travis's lap. "Oof. This girl is getting heavy."

Travis settled the baby in his lap and felt a surge of happiness at having her in his arms again. "She's growing up, that's all. She'll have a tooth soon, won't you, princess?"

Lizzie drooled and waved a fist at him.

"I know, I know. You want to finish your chow. Then we'll talk." He poked the bottle back in her eager mouth.

"Have you eaten?" Matty asked. "I'd be glad to fix you a plate."

Travis thought of the beautiful dinner Gwen had spent all day preparing and felt really sad that it had all gone to waste. He'd make it up to her. "That's okay," he said, gazing down at Lizzie as he gave her the bottle. His baby was getting prettier every day. He couldn't wait to see that first pearly tooth. "I'm not hungry, but I'd take a cup of coffee, if you have it."

"I'll get you one," Sebastian said. "Matty, tell him who called."

Travis looked up at her. "Yeah, who called?"

"Boone."

"He did?" Travis was pleased. Boone Connor was a hell of a nice guy, and Travis was always glad when summer came and the big blacksmith returned to the Rocking D from his hometown in New Mexico. "He must be about ready to head up here, huh? He needs to shoe the horses before—"

"He didn't call about shoeing horses," Matty said. She glanced down at the baby in Travis's lap.

Travis followed her gaze and a feeling of dread washed over him. Boone had been there that night in Aspen, too. Sebastian had said something about the call having to do with Jessica. Slowly his gaze rose to meet Matty's and his arm tightened instinctively around Lizzie. "Don't tell me he got a letter."

"Okay," Sebastian said as he set the mug of hot coffee in front of Travis. "Then I'll tell you. He got a letter."

"No way." Travis's stomach clenched. "This late?"

Sebastian sat down across from Travis. "He's been traveling all over with that horse-shoeing business and the letter just now caught up with him. He's headed up here."

Panic surged through Travis's heart. This was his

baby. His. Once he married Gwen, he'd be in a position to have custody. Matty and Sebastian could have visiting rights, of course. Generous visiting rights. "You're not going to tell me he thinks he's Lizzie's father. In that case we're talking Immaculate Conception. I think Boone's still a virgin."

"You'd better not say that to Boone. Remember how he was drinking and carrying on that night about feeling betrayed because his old girlfriend was getting married?"

"Yeah, and I think he lost that girl because he was too slow out of the gate. Next to the word *shy* in the dictionary is a picture of Boone Connor."

"He's not that bad," Sebastian protested. "Hell, I'm shy around women, myself."

Travis shook his head. "Boone's shy. You're clueless. There's a difference."

"A big difference," Matty said, laughing.

Travis leaned toward Sebastian. "I'd believe you were Lizzie's dad before I'd believe Boone was, and I don't believe you're even in the running."

"Watch it," Sebastian said.

Matty pushed back her plate. "You guys may not think it's true, but Boone is absolutely sure he slept with Jessica, first because drinking makes him act out of character and he drank a lot that night, and second because he was so broken up over his old girlfriend."

"Well, that's just bull!" Travis said.

Lizzie jerked in surprise at his loud tone.

"Whoops." Travis cuddled her closer. "Sorry, sweetheart. Daddy didn't mean to scare you."

"Careful how you throw that word around," Sebastian said with a slight edge to his voice.

"If the shoe fits," Travis said casually.

Sebastian glowered at him. "It fits me like a glove, as a matter of fact. I—"

"Boys!" Matty held up both hands. "I will not sit here and listen to another one of these idiotic arguments. I tremble to think what it's going to be like when Boone shows up. I might have to go stay with Gwen." She glanced at Travis. "And speaking of Gwen, where is she? And Luann? Isn't this your mother's last night here?"

Travis's chest grew tight and he kept his gaze on Elizabeth. "Yep."

"Uh...her last night, but you're here, not over there," Matty said. "I detect a problem."

"Oh, Matty, you're always detecting problems," Sebastian said. "Everything's fine, right, buddy?"

"Sure." Travis watched Lizzie drain the last of her bottle. He set it on the table and lifted the baby to his shoulder. "Couldn't be better."

"Oh, don't risk your shirt, Travis," Matty said quickly. "She's drooling like the dickens these days, and she'll mess up that black material. Sebastian, why don't you take Elizabeth? I think she needs to be changed." She glanced pointedly at Sebastian.

"Maybe Travis would like to change her," Sebastian said. "He hardly ever gets—"

"*Sebastian.*"

"On the other hand, I'd be more than happy to do it." He took the baby from Travis. "Come on, little one. Let's go find Bruce."

As he left, Matty leaned closer to Travis. "What happened?"

"Gwen asked her to move in permanently to Hawthorne House, and she said she'd rather hang by her teeth from the Royal Gorge Bridge."

"Oh, Travis." Sympathy shadowed Matty's blue eyes. "Did you try to talk to her about it?"

"Nope. And don't be telling me I should." A bitter taste returned to his mouth. "I've been dancing to that lady's tune for a long time, and if she's not willing to sacrifice a little bit for me, then I'm through with her."

Matty didn't say anything for a minute. Finally she spoke. "How'd Gwen take it?"

Travis sighed. "I'm sure she's upset. She wanted to try and talk my mother into changing her mind, but damn it, I don't want my mother there if she has to be dragged into it. She'll make me pay if that's the way it goes. Gwen doesn't get that."

"Did you fight with Gwen?"

"No. Yes." He looked away from Matty's direct gaze. "Sort of. But I'm sure she knows I'm not mad at her, just at my mother."

Matty reached over and squeezed his hand. Then she stood. "I'm going to drive into town and see Gwen."

Travis glanced up at her. "You're not thinking you'll talk my mother into staying, are you? Because I don't want you doing that. Not you or Gwen."

She patted his shoulder. "I won't try to talk your mother into staying. I just think Gwen could use a friend right now."

"She made a beautiful dinner," Travis said. "And we didn't get to eat it." Because he'd kissed Gwen and forced the issue, he thought sadly. But it would have come out the same in the end. His mother was insanely jealous, and she didn't want her perfect little life disturbed for anything or anyone.

"Tell Sebastian I'll be back in a couple of hours,"

Matty said. "And try not to get into a wrestling match with him over this kid while I'm gone."

DINNER WAS TUCKED into plastic containers in the refrigerator by the time Gwen opened the door and found Matty standing there.

"Got dessert?" Matty said with a grin.

"Oh, God, Matty. Travis must have driven to your place and told you what happened."

"He did."

Gwen hugged her friend tightly. "Thank you for coming. I've never been so glad to see anybody in my life."

Matty laughed and hung her jacket on the coat tree in the hall. "Oh, I wouldn't go that far. I'm sure you were more glad to see Travis earlier this week."

Gwen felt her cheeks warm as she remembered exactly what had gone on in the hall, right about where she and Matty were standing at this very moment. "It's a different kind of glad," she said.

"Let's hope so." Matty chuckled as she headed back toward the kitchen. "So, what did you make for dessert?"

"That better-than-sex chocolate cake you gave me the recipe for."

Matty groaned. "I knew it was calling me. Is it gone yet?"

"Gone? Why would it be gone?"

Matty sat at the kitchen table in her regular seat. "If I'd been the one dealing with this horse hockey, I probably would've eaten the whole thing by now."

Gwen smiled at her friend. "You're so good for me. I feel about a hundred percent better, already."

"Don't mention it. You've come through for me a time or two. So, where's Luann?"

"Upstairs in her room." Gwen looked up at the ceiling and grimaced. "She probably won't come down until she's ready to leave in the morning."

"I see. Well, first off I need to tell you that Boone Connor called and he got a letter asking him to be a godfather, too. He's on his way, ready to do his duty by this little girl he thinks is his."

Gwen sank onto a chair in amazement. "You're kidding."

"Don't I wish. Jessica has created a real mess. I'd love to get my hands on that woman."

Gwen shook her head. "Three men, all thinking they did the deed. Jessica had better show up fast."

"The detective is working on it, but Jessica's slippery. So anyway, I thought you should know about that little development."

"Thanks. I'm sure you told Travis." Gwen could just imagine Travis's reaction. He was becoming very possessive about the baby.

"I told him. He doesn't believe for one minute that Boone's the father, and neither does Sebastian. And I can guarantee Boone will fall in love with Elizabeth just the way the other two have. It'll be a circus around here." Matty looked hopefully over at the counter. "Um, are you gonna give me some cake?"

"You bet." Gwen didn't often forget her hostess duties, and she stood immediately, irritated with herself for being so absentminded after Matty had specifically indicated she wanted some dessert. Gwen crossed quickly to the counter and lifted the dome top from her cake platter.

"Sweet Lord in Heaven, that is a sight for sore

eyes," Matty said worshipfully. "You're gonna make some man a hell of a wife. Shoot, I wish you'd be *my* wife. With Sebastian for my husband and you for my wife, I'd be in high cotton."

Gwen laughed, but her heart wasn't in it. She cut a generous slice of cake for Matty. "You know, it's not going to work, me marrying Travis if he has this big rift with his mother. He thinks he can break off his relationship with her and just go on, but I know he can't. He loves her. And she loves him. I don't know what to do." She set the cake, a napkin and a fork down in front of Matty before taking a seat across from her.

Matty looked at her in surprise. "Where's your piece?"

"I'm not hungry."

"For *this?*" Matty hooted. "*Nobody's* not hungry for *this*. Get yourself some. It's therapy. And put the coffeepot on. We need to have us a brainstorming session."

Gwen sighed, but she got up and started the coffee brewing. Then she cut herself some cake and sat down at the table again. "It's no use. Travis doesn't want me to talk to his mother. And she leaves tomorrow, so there's really no time to change her mind, even if I thought I could sneak in a few conversations when Travis wasn't looking."

"We could both go up there right now, hold some cake just out of reach, and tell her she could have some if she'll be a good girl."

Gwen laughed. "That's better than anything I've come up with."

Matty took her first bite and rolled her eyes in ecstasy. She swallowed and cut another bite with her fork. "I swear, it would work. At least it would work on me. I'd clean the barn floor with a toothbrush if you promised me a piece of this cake at the end." She chewed and swallowed, then pointed at the cake with her fork. "I've made this, and it didn't taste half this good. You are one helluva cook."

"Thank you." Gwen took a bite of the cake, and it did taste pretty good. Chocolate was supposed to be a mood elevator. She took another bite.

"You could probably bring about world peace with this cake. I'm not kidding. You have a gift." Suddenly Matty paused, her fork in midair. "Maybe too much of a gift."

"Too much?"

Matty stared at Gwen. "God, that's it. I'm brilliant."

"I agree, but what brilliance are you guilty of this time?"

"No wonder Luann has a burr under her saddle. Tell me, did she expect you to wait on her hand and foot while she was here?"

"Not really. I wanted to do things for her." Gwen got up to pour them each a cup of coffee. "At first she insisted on helping out a little, but then, after Travis moved back into my bedroom I felt guilty about that, so I tried to make her stay even easier."

"So then you were doing it all."

"Pretty much." Gwen set a cup and saucer down by Matty's elbow. Then she brought over the sugar and poured cream into a favorite little flowered pitcher before putting that on the table, as well.

"Do you see that?" Matty pointed to the cream pitcher.

"Yeah, isn't it pretty? I found it in an antique shop in Colorado Springs, and I—"

"Not the pitcher, sweetie, the fact that you had to

put the cream in it instead of plopping the carton down on the table, like I'd do! You have this perfectionistic tendency that is so adorable, unless we're talking about your potential mother-in-law, who suddenly feels completely outclassed."

Gwen's mouth dropped open as she stared at Matty. "Outclassed? By me? That's ridiculous."

"Is it? You had this place spit-shined before she arrived. Then I'm sure you tried to keep it that way while she was here. I'm sure you fixed perfect meals and arranged beautiful bouquets for the table."

Gwen continued to stare at her friend.

Matty pointed a finger at her. "Didn't you?"

"Of course! She was my guest, and a very important guest. I wanted her to feel happy here. Special. I wanted her to think I'd be good enough for her son!"

"Oh, she knows you are. The problem is, she's become extraneous. I'll bet the only time she felt really needed was that day I schemed to have her baby-sit Elizabeth. She actually looked happy that day. She even cleaned my kitchen while she was there, which only proves my point. Around here she felt useless." Matty shot Gwen a look of triumph.

"But she wouldn't be useless if she lived here!" Gwen couldn't believe that Matty was right. "Surely she could figure out that I'd love to have her help with the business, and with the children, when we have them, and with—"

"Not if she thinks you can do everything better than she can. And you've proven how efficient and capable you are, so what purpose would she serve? Besides that, you'll make her look bad in front of her son. No way will she subject herself to that kind of comparison."

Gwen dropped her head in her hands and groaned. "I tried to make everything perfect, and all I did was screw it up. Now it's all ruined, and Travis and his mother are fighting, and they're both incredibly stubborn."

"I've decided all men are stubborn. So Luann must have more testosterone than most of us."

Gwen lifted her head with a faint smile. "Because we're never stubborn."

"Never." Matty grinned.

"But Matty, what am I going to do? No way can I turn this around in the next twelve hours. No way."

"I don't think so either."

"So I'm doomed?"

"Nope. Ordinarily I wouldn't approve of doing something like this, but we have a state of emergency, here."

Gwen allowed herself a small bit of hope. "I'll consider anything."

"You're sure? Because I have a feeling this will be very hard for you."

Gwen thought of all that was at stake and didn't hesitate. "Anything. I will be eternally grateful, Matty, for whatever you can think of to do."

"Forget the eternal gratitude. Just keep me supplied with cake."

16

AN HOUR LATER Gwen lay in bed under piles of blankets waiting for Travis to arrive. He showed up right on schedule. She heard his key rattle in the front door lock and then his boots hit the floor in quick strides as he hurried back to the bedroom.

He hesitated in the doorway. "Gwen? Honey, what's the matter? Matty said you weren't feeling good."

"I feel terrible," she said. "Chilled to the bone, upset stomach, bones aching."

He crossed quickly to the bed and crouched beside her. He laid the back of his hand against her cheek. "You're burning up. Must be the flu. I'll call Doc Harrison."

"Don't you dare. There's nothing they can do for the flu, anyway, except tell you to rest and drink fluids."

"It could be something worse." Travis's eyes clouded with worry. "What if it isn't just the flu?"

Gwen felt a surge of guilt for putting him through this. Matty had been right that it wouldn't be easy. Gwen rationalized by telling herself she did feel sick—heartsick. Or she had, before Matty had given her a plan.

"I'm sure it's nothing serious," she said. "But, listen, don't get too close, okay? I don't want you to catch it. You have to drive to Utah tomorrow."

"Fat chance. I'll put my mother on a Greyhound before I'll leave you when you're sick. And I don't care about getting sick. I want to take care of you. Do you need anything? Some juice? A back rub?"

She thought he looked entirely too eager to administer the back rub. "Oh, Travis, that's so sweet." She gave him what she hoped was a sickly smile. "But I can take care of myself. It's the guests, Bill and Charlene Ingram, I'm worried about. They arrive day after tomorrow."

"I'll call them and tell them the visit's off. It'll be just you and me. And the germs."

"You can't reach Bill and Charlene now." At least that much was true. "They're already on the road and they weren't sure where they'd stop on the way here because this trip is supposed to be spontaneous, except for their weekend at Hawthorne House."

Travis made an impatient noise in his throat. "If they're so spontaneous then they can find another place to stay this weekend."

"Oh, Travis, we can't ask them to do that. It's their first wedding anniversary. They spent their honeymoon here a year ago. I have a small piece of their wedding cake in the freezer."

Travis gazed at her, frustration shining in his golden eyes. "Look, sweetheart, I would be willing to do whatever I can, but you know I'm a lousy cook, and I'm even worse at arranging flowers and setting out hand towels and all those little things you do to make the house nice for people. And you can't be doing it. You won't feel like it, probably, and besides, you might give this bug to them, which wouldn't be very neighborly."

Gwen moaned. "Oh, Travis, I hate this. The Ingrams have been looking forward to their weekend for a whole year."

"I know, but stuff happens." He smoothed her forehead. "I'll help them find another place to stay. I'll call around."

"I wish I could think of another way. I wish..." She paused. "Travis, there is one solution. Oh, God, if only she'd be willing to help out."

"Who, Matty?"

"No, not Matty. She and Sebastian are going to buy cattle this weekend, remember? They're taking the baby."

"Yeah, that's right. I can't believe I forgot. So who were you thinking of?"

"Your mother."

"My *mother*?" He gave a short bark of laughter. "Oh, sure. That would work. Not. She can hardly wait to get out of here. I can't imagine her agreeing to hang around and cook and clean for your guests."

"You're probably right." Gwen sighed. "But it would solve everything if she'd just agree to stay a few more days. You could take care of me, and she could run the house temporarily."

Travis studied her. "You'd trust her to do that?"

"Of course I would." She'd never let him know how tough that was to say. Her little house was her domain, and she really wasn't looking forward to turning over the reins, but Matty had convinced her she had to if she ever expected to earn Luann's goodwill.

Travis rubbed his chin and looked thoughtful. "It would solve the problem, all the way around. When you're better, I could drive her home. No matter how mad she makes me, I wasn't looking forward to putting her on the bus. And a plane's no good, either. It'd only get her as far as Salt Lake City, and then she'd have to take a bus from there. She's not used to traveling alone."

"You'd be worried sick about her."

"Unfortunately." He grimaced. "I guess when it comes to her, my bark is worse than my bite."

"I thought as much." Gwen touched his hand. "At least ask her. If she turns you down, then we'll think of something else."

The muscles in his jaw tightened. "If she turns me down, I may put her on the bus after all."

LUANN DIDN'T TURN Travis down, and Gwen spent the next two days in bed trying not to go completely insane. She was bored out of her tree, which was bad enough, but even worse she had to lie there and listen to the sounds and scents of Luann cooking on her stove, washing her china, running her vacuum cleaner and dusting with her lemon polish. Matty had warned her she'd have trouble with that, and she definitely had trouble. The hardest pill to swallow was realizing that Luann seemed to be coping fine. Gwen wasn't indispensable.

Then she had to battle guilt again when Travis brought her a Ouija board as a "poor-me" present. But she had to smile at his choice. It was so Travis to bring her something to play with.

Immediately she suggested asking the Ouija board if he was Elizabeth's father. To her surprise he shook his head and told her she could ask the board anything else, but not that. His reluctance made her realize just how desperately he wanted the little baby to be his, and how ripe he was for a family of his own.

Although Travis looked in on her as much as possible in between trips to the Rocking D, part of Gwen's care fell to Luann. The first day she brought Gwen a bowl of soup for lunch with businesslike efficiency, but didn't pause to chat. Gwen would have complimented her on the soup, but it was her own, not Luann's.

On the second day Luann brought in another bowl of Gwen's soup, but she loosened up enough to ask if the patient was feeling any better.

"I feel really weak," Gwen said. Matty had advised her to stay bedridden for at least three days, and perhaps four, if she could stand it. The flu was supposed to leave you weak, Matty had said, so that was to be Gwen's standard line.

"Well, don't worry about a thing. We're all ready for your company," Luann said with a touch of pride.

"That's great." Gwen was dying to ask if Luann had made sure they had enough eggs in the refrigerator, and whether or not she'd put fresh flowers in the bedroom. But she didn't ask. Matty had given her strict instructions not to bring up those kinds of questions, which would make Luann think she wasn't trusted to do the job properly.

"I really appreciate this, Luann," she said instead. "When you run a business all by yourself, you never count on getting sick."

"I suppose not."

"And although Travis would be more than willing to help, he's not much good in this situation."

A small smile appeared briefly. "No, that boy doesn't know potpourri from potato chips."

Gwen had thought of one other little glitch. "Uh, Luann, I should probably warn you that the couple coming this afternoon has only been married a year. I can't guarantee that they won't make some—"

"I'll put cotton in my ears at night," she said. "Well, you rest now. I have banana bread to bake."

Not long afterward the aroma of banana bread drifted into Gwen's bedroom, making her mouth water. She'd had to pretend that she didn't have much of an appetite, but she was starving to death. At this rate she really would be weak—weak from hunger.

She gauged how long the banana bread had been in the oven and figured out when it would be done. From the way Luann had handled herself in the kitchen before Gwen had mistakenly insisted she needed to relax, Gwen had a hunch she was a pretty good cook.

The ding of the kitchen timer coincided with the sound of Luann bustling around. Gwen recognized those sounds well—Luann had set the bread out to cool. God, but it smelled good.

Finally she couldn't stand it another minute. Trying to keep her voice sounding like a sick person's, she called out to Luann.

Luann came to the door of her bedroom. "Is anything wrong?"

"No, nothing's wrong. I just...that bread smells heavenly. My appetite seems to be returning a little. Could I possibly have a slice?"

The expression on Luann's face was worth every blessed minute Gwen had spent languishing in that bed. Travis's mother beamed. Gwen had never seen her look like that, and it transformed her from the taut-faced woman who'd arrived with Travis to the loving mother Gwen had hoped Luann was underneath.

"Would you like a little butter on it?" Luann asked. She'd never addressed Gwen in such a sweet tone.

"I would love a little butter on it."

"And maybe a cup of that cinnamon tea?"

"That sounds perfect."

"Be right back." Luann hurried out, her step light.

Gwen closed her eyes in gratitude. "Thank you, Matty," she whispered.

GWEN STAYED in her suite Friday night and Saturday morning while Travis and Luann entertained the Ingrams. Judging from the laughter and happy voices, things were going well. Before Travis left for the Rocking D on Saturday he brought in a bouquet of flowers.

"These are from Bill and Charlene," he said as he set the vase down by her bed. "They hope you get better soon."

"How nice of them." She glanced into his eyes. "Everything's going okay, isn't it?"

Travis scratched the back of his head. "Yeah," he said with some surprise. "Yeah, it is. Damned if I can figure it out, either. When I asked Mom the other night if she'd do you this favor she acted as if it would be a huge imposition. But if I didn't know better, I'd say she's having a good time."

Gwen thought she should get an Oscar for the way she responded. Instead of punching a fist in the air as she longed to do, she merely nodded. "She's a good sport to pitch in, and she's saved my butt, that's for darn sure."

Travis crouched down beside the bed and combed her hair back from her face. "Feeling any better?"

"I am." *You have no idea.* "But I don't think I should push it. Maybe tomorrow, after the Ingrams leave, I'll try getting out of bed for a while."

Travis gazed at her tenderly. "You've always been such a can-do lady. I sure didn't want you to come down with the flu, but it makes me feel all macho and protective to know that you need help, sometimes, too. In some ways, that's been a nice feeling. Not that I want you to get sick again, ever," he added quickly.

Gwen was startled. "Don't tell me you thought I was invincible...?" She caught herself before she added the word *too*.

"I guess I did." He stroked her cheek with his thumb. "I knew how much I needed you, but I wasn't sure you really needed me."

"You're kidding."

He grinned, but his eyes remained serious. "Well, aside from the sex."

She pressed his hand against her cheek and her heart swelled with love for him. "Oh, Travis, sex is only part of it. I need you to talk with me, work beside me, laugh with me. Especially that last part. I thought you knew that."

"I didn't. Not really. But I do now," he said softly.

"I love you."

"I love you, too," he murmured. Then he stood and leaned over her to kiss her on the forehead. "Rest now. I want you to get well." He waggled his eyebrows at her. "And you might as well know my motives aren't pure, either."

"You want a fresh batch of cinnamon rolls?"

He laughed. "You know how much I love those things."

"Oh, I do."

"But on the list of what I'm hungry for, they run a very distant second." He winked and left the room.

Gwen lay there and battled extreme sexual frustration. Not only had she been forced to turn over her house to Luann, she'd had to pretend she wasn't interested in making love to Travis. One lusty response on her part and he'd have suspected she'd been pretending to have the flu.

She still wasn't sure how they'd made it through the times he'd helped her shower and wash her hair. He'd fought his arousal with such determination, and she'd felt like such a fraud. Yet apparently he'd benefitted from her fake illness as much as Luann had. Someday she'd tell him the truth about this weekend, but not yet, not when so much was still hanging in the balance.

Once the Ingrams were gone, Gwen planned to make a big deal about Luann's help during the crisis and drop some heavy hints about how much easier it would be to run a bed and breakfast if two women lived here. And it would be, Gwen admitted grudgingly, although she hadn't come to that conclusion without a struggle. Staying in this bed had taught her some things, too. She wondered if Matty had intended that it should.

Giving up control of her house had been one of the toughest things she'd ever done, but now she knew she could. And with luck, so did Luann.

Travis called late in the afternoon to say a waterline had sprung a leak at the ranch and fixing it would make him late getting home. The Ingrams had gone out for their anniversary dinner, and Gwen was still playing sick and eating small meals from a bed tray.

To Gwen's delight, Luann chose to eat her dinner in

Gwen's bedroom. During the meal the older woman
was positively chatty, talking easily about gardening,
cleaning projects and recipes. Gwen couldn't believe
the change. She also realized how much she appreci-
ated this kind of conversation, one she could never
have with her own mother. Even Matty wasn't into
domestic topics that much, but Luann cared about the
same things Gwen did. For the first time Gwen began
to think of Luann as a bonus instead of a burden. It
was a liberating thought.

Gwen wasn't sure how long Luann would have
stayed to talk, but Travis came home, tired and hungry, and she hurried to the kitchen to heat up his food.
Gwen half expected him to bring his plate into the
bedroom, too, but instead she heard chairs scrape in
the kitchen, as if he and his mother had sat down at
the kitchen table.

For one unworthy moment Gwen felt jealous. Then
the moment passed. After all, she'd been working toward this very goal, mending the rift between mother
and son. If they were choosing to talk alone in the
kitchen, then she'd accomplished her mission. But she
was dying to know what they were talking about. And
who.

She pulled her Ouija board out from under the bed
and set it on her lap. With the plastic piece under her
fingertips she silently asked who the conversation was
about. Sure enough, it slid across the alphabet to spell
out her name.

Damn, but she wanted to hear what they were saying! Yet she couldn't very well lurk at the door. If
Travis came back in, she'd never make it back to the
bed without him catching her. She put the board away
and snuggled down into the covers.

Travis and Luann's voices were hushed, and she couldn't make out words at all. She'd just have to trust Travis to be diplomatic in his dealings with his mother, the way she'd had to trust Luann to take good care of her house guests. She heaved a sigh. Another lesson to learn.

Still she couldn't help straining to hear. Finally the attempt to make out words amidst the steady drone of voices had a hypnotic effect, and she must have dozed off, because the next thing she knew the bedside light snapped off and Travis crawled into bed with her.

She turned sleepily to give him a good-night kiss. He kissed her back and there was so much restrained energy in that kiss that her eyes popped open. "Travis? Is everything all right?"

His whole body seemed to hum as he gathered her close. His voice was rich and deep in her ear. "She wants to stay."

Gwen gasped and looked into his shadowed face. "She *does?*" She'd never in her wildest dreams imagined that Luann would capitulate of her own accord.

"She wants me to ask you if the offer is still open."

Gwen let out a whoop of triumph.

"Hey." Travis chuckled. "Don't get too excited. You might trigger a relapse."

Barely in time Gwen remembered her role. She coughed several times, as if the whoop had really taken the starch out of her.

"See?" Travis rubbed her back. "Look what you've done. Want some water?"

"No. No, thanks." Her body warmed to his touch. "Oh, Travis, how wonderful. I'm thrilled that she wants to stay."

"Me, too." He continued to stroke her back. "I hate to say this, but it's probably because you got sick."

"*Really.*"

"Yeah. She admitted to me tonight that until that happened, she didn't think there was a place for her here. But now she realizes what a drain this place can be on one woman. She can see that you really do need her if you're going to try and run a bed and breakfast and raise a family, too."

"And she's so right!" Gwen snuggled against him. His muscular body felt so good pressed against hers. He'd worn a T-shirt and briefs to bed, as he'd been doing the entire time she'd been pretending to be sick. She wanted the underwear off.

Travis sighed and held her close, resting his cheek against the top of her head in an almost brotherly fashion. She gritted her teeth.

"Thank God she came to her senses," he said. "I was trying to imagine our wedding without her there. It made me sort of sick to my stomach."

"And now she can help us plan it." Gwen envisioned the fun she and Luann would have making this an event to remember. And then would come the honeymoon. Gwen could hardly wait for that part.

"Oh, she wants to help plan it. But I warned her I'm looking for speed, here. Two weeks, tops."

"Two weeks?" She raised her head to look up at him. "That's not nearly enough time."

"With you two on the job? It's more than enough time, unless you think it'll be tough on you, just getting over being sick and all."

She rubbed her body against his. "That won't be a problem. I'm practically well."

"But not completely. Stop that."

She slipped a hand up under his T-shirt. "I think I'm well enough."

"I don't know about this, Gwen."

"I do." She felt his nipples tighten under her caressing palm. "And I'll bet you'd like to."

"Uh...it's possible." His breathing grew labored. "Maybe we could try it, if we only use the missionary position and I'm very careful with you."

Her heart raced and her body moistened just thinking about making love in some position, any position at all. "I think we could risk it."

"Okay." His voice was husky. "Easy now." He rolled her slowly to her back and slid his hand under her sensible cotton nightgown. "After being sick for so long, you may be a little slow to..." He sucked in a breath as he encountered her moist heat. "Then again, maybe not." As he stroked her beneath the gown, his breathing grew ragged. "Maybe I should leave this on, so you don't catch a chill."

She wanted that nightgown gone. In fact, she'd be willing to burn it. "Let's take it off and then I'll put it back on, afterward."

"If you're sure."

"With it on, I might become overheated."

"Oh! I didn't think of that. Well, then we should take it off." He stopped caressing her long enough to work her nightgown carefully over her head. "Still okay?"

"Peachy. What about your clothes?" She reached for the elastic of his briefs.

"I'll do it." He slipped out of his briefs and took his T-shirt off over his head. "You're only supposed to lie there and enjoy."

"Yes, sir." She quivered with anticipation.

"You're shivering. Are you cold?"

"No. Yes. If you cover me with your body I'll stay warm."

"I can do that." He started to move over her. "Wait. I need to get a con—"

"I don't think you do."

He went very still. "I don't?"

"Didn't you say two weeks?"

"Or less."

"Then why bother with those silly things any more?"

A fine tremor passed through him. "Cover your eyes," he said at last. "I'm turning on the light."

"Okay." She put her hand over her eyes as he leaned over to switch on the lamp. Slowly she uncovered her eyes to find him looking down at her with more focus and intensity than ever before. "Why did you want the light?" she asked.

His gaze never leaving hers, he moved over her. "Because I want to be able to look into your eyes while I make you pregnant with our baby."

Desire swept through her. With a moan she grasped his hips and urged him forward.

He resisted her. "No. I'm taking this slow."

"You don't have to." She was wild to have him inside her. "I'm really okay now."

"I believe you. I'm taking it slow because I want to remember this moment for the rest of my life." And with that he gradually eased into her, the flame in his eyes growing brighter and brighter, until at last he was settled, deep and secure within her.

He gazed into her eyes. No doubt about it. He was giving her *The Look*. "Forever," he murmured.

Joyfully she took the promise into her heart. They

would have a ceremony someday soon, with a minister and all of their loved ones, and she knew it would be beautiful and moving and important. But it would only be a formality.

Tonight they would exchange their vows.

She cupped his face in her hands. "Forever," she whispered.

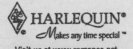

Romance is just one click away!

online book serials

➤ *Exclusive* to our web site, get caught up in both the daily and weekly online installments of new romance stories.

➤ Try the Writing Round Robin. Contribute a chapter to a story created by our members. Plus, winners will get prizes.

romantic travel

➤ Want to know where the best place to kiss in New York City is, or which restaurant in Los Angeles is the most romantic? Check out our Romantic Hot Spots for the scoop.

➤ Share your travel tips and stories with us on the romantic travel message boards.

romantic reading library

➤ Relax as you read our collection of Romantic Poetry.

➤ Take a peek at the Top 10 Most Romantic Lines!

Visit us online at

www.eHarlequin.com
on Women.com Networks

COMING NEXT MONTH

#785 MOONLIGHTING Heather MacAllister
Sweet Talkin' Guys

Amber Madison had always had a weakness for sweet-talkin'
Logan Van Dell. Years ago he'd even charmed her into running
away with him—then he'd left her to go on alone. Now Amber is
home, and Logan's just as irresistible. During their moonlight
trysts, Amber can't help falling for him all over again. But will
Logan still be around when the sun comes up?

#786 SAWYER Lori Foster
The Buckhorn Brothers, Bk. 1

The day Honey Malone—fleeing from a dangerous predator—
drove her car into a lake, she found herself up to her neck in
gorgeous men! After Sawyer Hudson—Buckhorn's only doctor—
and his three bachelor brothers nursed her through her injuries,
she tried to leave. But she hadn't bargained on the stubborn
protectiveness of the Buckhorn Brothers.

#787 TOO HOT TO SLEEP Stephanie Bond
Blaze

Georgia Adams couldn't sleep...and it wasn't because of the local
heat wave. She had a lukewarm boyfriend, a nonexistent love
life...and she was frustrated, *really* frustrated. Deciding to heat
things up, she phoned her boyfriend for a little phone
flirtation...and a lot more. Her bold experiment was wildly
successful. Only, Georgia didn't realize she'd dialed the wrong
number....

#788 BOONE'S BOUNTY Vicki Lewis Thompson
Three Cowboys & A Baby

Shelby McFarland and her three-year-old nephew, Josh, were on
the run. When a snowstorm left them stranded, Shelby thought
the game was over...until a strong, sexy cowboy rescued them.
Boone Connor made Shelby feel safe, protected—and very, very
desired. They'd make a perfect family—only, Boone already had a
baby....